HOLIDAY FACE-OFF

PUCK BATTLE SERIES

BOOK ONE

KRISTEN ECHO

Holiday Face-off
Puck Battle Series Book One
Copyright © 2017 by Kristen Echo and Kristen
Publishing
All rights reserved.

This book is a work of fiction. Names, characters, places, and incidents are the product of the author's imagination or are used fictitiously. Any resemblance to actual events, locales, or persons, living or dead, is coincidental.

Website: www.echoromance.com
Facebook: www.facebook.com/authorkristenecho

Cover Design: Rebecacovers

ISBN 978-0-9952712-3-4
eBook ISBN 978-0-9952712-2-7

This one is for my girls.
Always follow your dreams.

ACKNOWLEDGMENTS

Thanks to all the new friends I've made during my foray into publishing, especially the folks in the online writer groups I've joined. We are making it happen one book at a time. The writing community is full of amazing people who are willing to share their knowledge with the minnows like me. This hockey series continues because of all the help and advice I've received along the way.

A special thank you to my street team for your fabulous feedback and for being in my corner. Eryn, Cynthia, Linda, and Laurette, your words mean more than I can express and I am truly grateful. I absolutely love my book covers and they wouldn't be so brilliant without Rebeca's talent. She saw my vision and made it happen. Rebecacovers you are amazing! This book took a completely different direction thanks to my editor Michael Pilgrim. Thank you for giving me the hard truth. I valued your feedback and feel like this book is stronger and hotter thanks to your feedback.

As always, my thanks to my family for their enduring support. I love you with all my heart, forevermore.

Big Hugs
&
Happy reading to all!

CHAPTER ONE

It sucked being single at Christmas. The holidays could be a lonely time of year even when by choice. Carly Saint had her reasons, but that didn't make the ache in her chest any less real.

A snowflake from the darkened sky landed on her nose. The sun wasn't due to make an appearance for another hour. With any luck, it would push the storm clouds away. Thirty percent chance of flurries. For once she wanted the weatherman to be right. She needed him to be right.

The city looked festive and peaceful on her drive to work. Snow blanketed every inch with shimmering sparkles. A winter wonderland that Carly couldn't appreciate yet. Not until her shift at the diner was over and she was sailing thousands of feet in the air would she get to enjoy the beauty of the Christmas season.

There were no cars on the road as she drove outside the city limits. She lived in the campus dorms, but worked at a rural diner because it reminded her of home. She could have worked on campus like everyone else, but not with that hectic pace. Plus, she fell in love with the owners the first time she set foot in the fifties style truck stop diner. In six months of employment, this was the first time she wished it was closer to school.

Every direction was snow covered prairies and white, frosted buildings. The snow made the road slick, forcing her to drive slow. Thirty minutes became an hour. Despite the icy conditions, she arrived on time.

She popped into the back office to punch the clock. "Morning, Carly. Thanks again for taking this shift," Mr. Richardson said when he spotted her tying her apron. "You look nice today."

She had styled her shoulder length hair into a messy ponytail with cascading tendrils around her face. A touch of light make-up and heavy mascara completed the effortlessly chic look. Unfortunately, she couldn't say the same for the black t-shirt and blue jeans uniform.

Perry Richardson was a kind boss who noticed small details others overlooked. The compliment made her blush. He looked like a younger version of Santa Claus. Exchange the brown beard for white and he was a shoe in for the job. When he asked for something, like working on Christmas eve, she felt compelled to help.

"Um… Thanks and no problem; my flight isn't until five thirty." Her shift ended at two thirty, leaving her enough time to make it to the airport even with poor conditions. She leaned over his desk to peek out the window for a view of the near empty parking lot, praying the snow would stop. It hadn't.

Mr. Richardson settled into his chair and switched on the small TV which hung on the wall by his desk. "This is your first visit back in a while, right?"

The news broadcasted the face of a missing teen. Lately, it seemed as though a new face was being shown every week. Criminals were taking over, giving Carly an uneasy feeling. He flipped through the channels until he reached the sports network.

City crime rates were at an all-time high, providing another reason to head back to her small northern Saskatchewan home town. A place she'd been happy to leave at the start of summer. It's not like she had extra time to spare or the money to go back, but her parents expected her home for the holidays.

"Yup." She hoped her curt response would stop the questions.

"Your folks must be happy to get you home." The statement hung in the air, making Carly question the reality of it. "They still on your case about the ex?"

Mrs. Richardson loved to gossip. The nice older woman was like a second mother, and Carly appreciated having her shoulder to cry on when they first met. Only her secrets weren't secrets for long. Everyone heard she had an ex from hell, and parents who worshiped him.

She plastered on her fake smile; the one she'd perfected for customers. It oozed charm with a dash of sass, but also said don't mess with me. "Things are fine. Thank you for asking." She switched her focus to the thirty-inch flat screen. Carly wondered how he got any work done with the distraction. Highlights of last night's hockey game were being shown.

"Did you catch the game?" He asked, and she was happy for the change in subject. She was a hockey fan. One of the few things they had in common.

"Sure did, we slaughtered the Penguins. If we keep this up, we may have a shot at playoffs." Carly couldn't skate to save her life, but still loved to watch the game. Her father was a diehard Jets fan and his love rubbed off on her at some point.

The points flashed across the screen. The night's top spot went to Theo Montagne; last year's Rookie of the Year. The announcers showed last night's hat-trick. Not his first of the season. Each of his three goals looked effortless. He had serious talent. They displayed a picture of Theo with his wild mop of brown hair, piercing blue eyes and killer smile. Carly stared at the picture, tuning out the announcer's commentary.

"Good looking kid, don't you think?" Mr. Richardson's question caught her off guard. "Looks like a nice guy too."

She didn't know how to answer. Yes, the man was attractive, okay smoking hot, but he was also a hockey player which she found unappealing. "If you like hockey players, I guess." She shrugged her shoulders. "I'll be up front if you need me. Try not to work too hard, boss." Carly winked and finished signing in. As much as she hated gossip, she loved the owners like family.

Mr. Richardson nodded, shuffling papers on his desk. "Don't leave today without coming to say bye. The Mrs. and I got you a little something." Carly put her hands out, hoping to get whatever the present was now. Chocolate was always welcomed since her sweet tooth was never satisfied. He swatted them away. "After shift; don't forget."

"Sure, I won't forget." Carly would never leave chocolate behind. She closed the office door and made her way up front. Those two were so generous, another reason she worked out in the middle of nowhere.

As expected, there weren't many customers when the doors opened. A slow morning meant few tips. The shift was a favor, but in reality, she didn't mind. She needed every penny. Plane tickets nearly doubled around the holidays, but going back was important. She felt guilty enough for choosing a school that was thousands of miles away. She didn't want to add yet another disappointment in their eyes.

Her parents acted like they were happy with her decisions, but she could tell they wanted their only child closer. They supported her with bright smiles, which only made her feel worse. Behind the fake grins, she was breaking their hearts. She stuffed those thoughts away as the hustle and bustle of serving customers picked up.

"Don't look so glum, your tips suffer when you're not smiling," Miranda said with a big ear to ear grin. Her co-worker didn't have to remind Carly of that fact.

Her shift was coming to an end and the small amount of change jingling in her apron was enough of a reminder. She forced a toothy grin. They were getting harder to fake as the day progressed. She wanted to go home, but dreaded seeing certain people.

"Why are you so cheerful?" Most people were delighted that Christmas eve had finally arrived, but Carly knew Miranda's big smile had nothing to do with the holidays.

"Chuck surprised me last night with an after-game hat-trick of his own. A three orgasms performance. And then again this morning. I am one lucky lady."

Carly sputtered the coffee she'd snuck a sip of. Miranda had no filter. "OMG. Keep it down! I'm not sure the tables in the back heard ya." Carly giggled.

Miranda's husband was another Jets fan who took the game too seriously. He played the sport in a rec league and thought he was God's gift to women.

Every hockey player she'd ever met thought that way. On more than one occasion she'd debated the merits of dating hockey players with Miranda. Carly wasn't convinced they weren't all egotistical maniacs with daddy issues.

"Hush yourself. If the team keeps playing this good I might end up pregnant before Easter." Miranda rubbed her flat stomach.

The couple wanted a baby but according to Mrs. Richardson; Chuck was a cheater. Miranda confirmed as much the last time she worked. Men like Chuck fueled Carly's bitterness.

"Sounds like you've patched things up then? Last time we spoke, you were kicking his lying ass out?" It was impossible to mask the irritation in her voice. Chuck didn't cheat habitually, which made him more faithful than any other hockey player she had ever known.

Miranda bit her lip and looked down. "I was angry when we talked. Chuck explained everything. It was all one huge misunderstanding, and we're all good now."

Carly wasn't sure who she was trying to convince. "How exactly did he explain the fact that he had sex with someone other than his wife?" She kept her voice low to keep their conversation private, but she wanted to scream. Cheating was unforgivable. It had happened to her, and she vowed it would never happen again.

Miranda straightened her apron and came closer. "You've met Chuck. My man's easy on the eyes and a damn good hockey player. No one can handle a stick like he can." She waggled her brow and Carly wanted to hide under the counter. "There is nothing to explain and I don't want to talk about the past. He promised it—."

"Would never happen again. And you believe him?" Carly believed Chuck deserved to be benched; permanently.

"Don't give me that look, Miss Saint. I'm not an idiot, but I do love him. He's a good man and I'm not interested in becoming a thirty-year-old divorced woman, searching for love again. When you find the right one, you'll see what I mean. You'll grab on with both hands and never let go. He'll make you think anything is possible. Besides, I want to start a family, and Chuck promised me a happy life. Today, I am a happy woman. When was the last time you said that?"

It had been a long while since Carly had allowed herself that kind of happiness. "We're not talking about me. If you're happy, then I am too." She truly meant her words. Carly lived vicariously through her friends. She just hoped he'd keep his promise this time.

"Thanks. Your prince is out there too. A man who can make you come so hard you'll be seeing stars, my girl. Hey, maybe we'll have babies around the same time. Christmas miracles happen all the time." She winked before sauntering off to clear a table.

An ache in her chest nearly stopped her heart. Her hand moved to her stomach as she took a few deep breaths, but it left her off kilter. Carly doubted her friend; she didn't deserve the kind of miracle Miranda mentioned.

There wasn't much time to dwell on her conversation since customers came in to get out of the storm. The lunch rush had Carly hopping. Most of their clients were truckers and nearing the end of her shift the place was packed.

"Double espresso," a deep, male voice said.

Carly looked up from the register into the face of none other than Mr. Hockey-Star himself, Theo Montagne. She rubbed her eyes, thinking she had to be mistaken because celebrities never came to the diner. But he was real and standing inches from her. Her thighs clenched, and her cheeks blushed. She gulped. He was even more attractive up close and personal than he was on the TV screen.

CHAPTER Two

Her heart fluttered at the sight of him, which ticked her off. Good looks and money didn't make him more special or significant than any other customer. Thick, dark brown locks fell across his forehead shielding his eyes. Even without seeing the crystal-clear pools of blue, she recognized him. He shook the melting snow off his black baseball cap before quickly putting it back on and pulling the brim low to hide his identity.

Carly suspected he wasn't in the mood for a fan moment, though her heart beat a mile a minute in his presence. She'd never been this close to someone famous before. Hockey player or not, he was a customer. She flashed an extra-large smile, not that it mattered. He didn't look up from his phone. Arrogance rolled off him in waves.

"Feel free to grab any vacant table, although there aren't many left." She pointed around the diner, but his eyes remained glued to his phone. Carly rolled her eyes and hoped he sat at one of Miranda's tables.

Miranda wasn't the only lover of hockey players. Carly's roommate would swoon if she was this close to Theo Montagne. Beth had an addiction to hockey and an unhealthy attraction to hockey players. The past six months, Carly watched her date four different hockey players. All of whom used and tossed her aside like a piece of garbage. Beth was a sweet girl, but her fixation on the sport clouded her judgment regarding the men.

Being an athlete didn't give these guys the right to treat people like crap. Her own dating history revealed similar conduct. They treated women as though they were lucky to have a moment of their time. Beth was on a mission to marry a hockey player. She had a list of men from the National Hockey League she planned to seduce. Theo Montagne was on that list.

"Do I order here or at the table?" The hockey player asked. The deep timbre of his voice sent shivers down Carly's spine.

"Depends which table you take. If you take the only one open next to the window, then I can take your order now, otherwise you'll have to wait for the other waitress to get to ya." She could have kicked herself for not directing him towards the two empty tables on the left.

She didn't want to serve him, right?

"Thanks. I was kidding about the espresso by the way." He smiled, his straight white teeth sparkled like the freshly fallen snow. Carly wished he'd look up but he kept his head down. "I'd like a cup of coffee and the lunch special, please."

At least this ego maniac was polite. "Sure thing."

Carly smiled again, but her efforts were in vain.

The hockey player walked away, never having looked at her once. He was a tall guy without being imposing. Carly admired his broad build. Over six feet of lean muscles lay hidden under a black leather jacket. Carly punched his order into the system and watched him from the corner of her eye. He had the most firm and round ass she'd seen in ages. Her mouth salivated as he flaunted that perfect behind, making his way to the table in her section and disappearing from her view.

It was a shame he never noticed her. He couldn't be bothered to acknowledge her existence, which didn't surprise her even though it stung.

If he was too busy to spare her a glance, then he could wait for his caffeine fix. Carly was busy too. She checked on her other tables and waited another minute before fetching his cup of coffee. When she approached his table, he typed on his phone with purpose. Whatever conversation he was having must have been important. His full lips thinned into a straight line and his jaw clenched as he concentrated on the device in his hands. He had huge hands, making the phone seem tiny by comparison.

Carly wondered what it would feel like to have those big paws on her. Touching her in places she hadn't been touched in far too long. Would they be rough or gentle?

She cleared her suddenly dry throat. The coffee felt too warm in her hands and her face became rosy. She placed his cup on the table in front of him with yet another smile that was not returned. Theo mumbled a word of thanks, effectively dismissing her.

Leaning against the counter, she wondered why

she cared if he looked at her or not. It's not like he would fall in love at first sight like in the movies. But damn it, she wanted to get a peek at those stunning blue eyes she'd seen on TV.

"How are you still standing upright, girl?" Miranda asked, leaning next to her, fanning her face.

"What?" Carly's cheeks heated as she turned to face her co-worker. She tucked a few loose curls behind her ears before tugging on the hem of her black t-shirt. The uniform shrunk in the dryer, exposing a tiny slice of midriff on the sides where the apron didn't cover.

"Theo Montagne talked to you, and your knees didn't buckle. What's wrong with you?" She giggled like a school girl.

Anyone who knew anything about hockey would be able to recognize him. Hat or no hat, he was a big deal around these parts. He was that good on the ice, and judging by the size of those giant hands, he was good off it as well. His first-year points beat records created by some of the greats. His second season was more of the same. Drafted right after high school, he wasn't much older than Carly. He could retire tomorrow with more zeros in his bank account than anyone needed in a lifetime.

None of that impressed her. "He barely said more than two words. Hardly a swoon worthy encounter."

Judging by the look on Miranda's face, she thought otherwise. "Girl, are you telling me he didn't flirt shamelessly with you like all the other men here? Your wholesome face and rocking body keeps this place packed."

The diner was busy because the food was

amazing, not because of Carly's looks. "You're exaggerating. He didn't even look at me, so flirting was out of the question." A model, she wasn't. But most of the male clientele commented on her curves and some even asked her out. She turned them all down for several reasons, but mostly because she wanted to focus on her studies. She considered herself pretty enough to catch a man's eye, except she couldn't catch Theo's.

"But you admit he's hot, right?"

Carly thought about the question and nodded. Theo Montagne might not be someone she would ever consider dating, but she could appreciate a good-looking man. "He's attractive, but cocky. Not my type."

Miranda bumped her hip and leaned in close next to her ear. "Hon, he's everyone's type. If I had some mistletoe... I would go get me a kiss."

Carly wouldn't turn down a kiss either, but Mr. Hockey wouldn't notice her even if she slapped him in the face with the stuff. It's not like she expected the guy to drool at her feet after seeing her, but it would have been nice to at least catch a glimpse of his baby blues. Her pride took a slight beating at his lack of response, but she pushed the hurt aside.

Big deal, a famous hockey player showed up and ignored her, so what?

"Good thing we're out of mistletoe," Carly said and both girls laughed. Their conversation was cut short when two new customers approached the counter. Something about them gave Carly the creeps. Miranda grabbed a coffee pot and took off.

One of the men towered over her. Everything about this guy screamed danger. "That's a shame, you ain't got more mistletoe, since a kiss from you would make my day, sweet cheeks." The overweight man appeared to be in his early forties with yellowing teeth and a twisted smile.

The pickup line wasn't a welcomed one, but she smiled anyway. "Happy holidays. Are you staying or getting something for the road?" She hoped he would get what he needed and leave. She had no desire to chitchat with this guy or his friend.

"Well, we were gonna hit the road, but you've convinced us to stay."

She was afraid he would say that. "Grab a table and someone will be with you shortly." She gestured to the empty table near the back, which happened to be in Miranda's section. This was one time she wouldn't have minded being invisible.

"We'll sit up here at the counter, so we can be closer to you," the shorter man said in a thick accent Carly couldn't decipher. He removed his gloves and placed them on the counter. They were covered in scratches, like he had been holding a cat against its will and the beast had clawed for freedom and lost. Poor cat.

They were most likely bored and lonely truckers. She plastered on a smile and remembered that tips were better when she wasn't snarky. "Great choice. What can I get for you today?"

"This holiday would be a happy one for sure if I had someone sweet like you to share it with." The taller man raised his brows suggestively. He leaned over the counter, getting closer than she was comfortable with, and eyed her from top to bottom. The men smelled like leather and menace combined. He licked his chapped lips, making her cringe inside.

"We could make this a Christmas you'll never forget. What time are you done here?"

Carly shuffled her feet, wanting to get the last thirty minutes of her shift over with. "I'm not on the menu." The words popped out. She quickly added. "My shift ends soon. Perhaps the candy cane hot chocolate would be to your liking since you want something sweet. It is on sale too. The lunch special is also a hit; a Ruben with fries and coleslaw. Are you wanting to place a food order?" She couldn't get the words out fast enough. The sooner she took their order the faster she could get away.

A quick glance left and her eyes landed on Theo Montagne as he walked past, presumably on his way to the washroom. The smirk painted on his face, rubbed her the wrong way. He was no doubt laughing at her discomfort. Jerk.

The imposing man laughed as though she'd said something comical. Carly tensed as she returned her focus on him. He scratched the dark stubble on his chin, keeping his shady, almost black, beady eyes on her. "Relax, sweet cheeks, I'll take two extra-large coffees to go. Throw in a couple of cinnamon buns since we've got a few errands to run before we can celebrate the holidays."

She rushed to fill their order. Something about them didn't sit well with her. The way they watched her as she worked, like they were assessing her. She handed them the two cups, and they both made a few more lewd and inappropriate remarks before paying.

Customers flirted all the time, some taking it a little too far, but these two took it a step past gross. She sometimes flirted back, but this time the thought never crossed her mind to try.

Some Christmas this was turning out to be. Carly breathed a sigh of relief when the door closed behind them. She was used to seeing all walks of life come into the diner and most were harmless. These men were the opposite of innocent.

The bell rang from the kitchen, signaling an order for pickup. She raced to the warming tray and grabbed the hockey player's plate. Most of her tables were done and soon her shift would be over.

His brown hair curled around the edges of his hat. The flush to her cheeks returned. There was something so casually sexy about him. Too bad he was a hockey player, because he fit her type perfectly. She put his plate down on the table. His nose was buried in his phone as it had been before. "One special. Can I top up your coffee or get you anything else?"

"More coffee would be great, thanks." He put down his phone but only to pick up his sandwich. "Oh, Miss?"

"Yeah." She straightened her stance, waiting for him to continue.

"Never mind." He kept his head down and took a bite.

Not a single glance was sent her way. Without knowing it, this man was getting under her skin. She refilled his cup in silence and left him to eat. She slipped his bill on the table in the process. The less she had to deal with him the better.

Carly glanced at the clock and smiled her first genuine smile of the day. One last table to clear and she was done for an entire week. Soon she would be home for the holidays and she'd be able to put the flutters and Theo Montagne out of her mind.

CHAPTER THREE

One of the regulars sang an off-key version of Let It Snow as he pointed at the window. Sure, the ice crystals made for a lovely picture-perfect Christmas, the kind you see trapped in snow globes, but she wished for clear skies.

She needed chocolate, that always made everything better. Carly looked at the sea of couples around the diner with envy as she cashed out. They cuddled with their loved ones, basking in the holiday ambiance. The place had garland, large candy canes and tinsel covering every square inch. The aftermath resembled Santa's workshop.

As a little girl, Carly loved this time of year. The lights, the presents and spending extra time with her family. The holidays were all about family, reminding her of how lonely she'd become.

An attempt to deliver her goodbyes with a simple happy holiday, and escape without getting embraced by each of her co-workers failed. Her boss gave her a generous Christmas bonus. Two hundred bucks wasn't a big deal to some, but to Carly it meant the world. She hugged Mr. and Mrs. Richardson so hard they had to pry her off. She was overwhelmed by their generosity and she became teary eyed. The ordeal took longer than expected, leaving her little wiggle room if she wanted to make her flight on time.

The weather had taken a turn for the worse as the buckets of snow continued to fall. Once she stepped outside, she realized the amount was far more than she'd expected. So much for thirty percent. The hairs on the back of her neck raised as though she was being watched. She dismissed it, thinking it was the storm.

A tiny cherry red sports car was parked so close to her truck she could barely squeeze by. At least she thought she saw hints of red under the mountain of snow it was buried beneath. She opened her truck door enough to reach in and grab the snow brush. The car engine next to her roared to life, startling Carly. She jerked upright and smacked her head against the door frame. The hood fell from her head and she reached to massage the newly formed bump.

Carly wasn't usually the jumpy type. Nothing seemed to go according to plan today. She turned her back to the parking lot and went to work, brushing the snow off the windshield and wishing her old truck had command start. The temperature was well below freezing, but there was no place to plug in. She gave up the fight to clear the snow when she realized there was no keeping up with the deluge.

The crunching of snow under heavy boots caught her attention. She turned and noticed the two disturbing men from earlier coming towards her. The sinister smiles on their ugly faces looked anything but friendly. They should have been long gone, instead their long strides brought them closer than they had reason to be.

"Hey, sweet-cheeks, we forgot to give you your tip," the taller man said, closing the gap between them. "We've got a fistful of mistletoe."

A lump formed in Carly's throat, preventing her from responding or screaming. Considering how busy the diner and adjacent gas station were, Carly couldn't see anyone else outside. She looked around, but it was only the three of them, and they were getting closer.

She felt trapped. There was nowhere to go. Her grip on the brush tightened, she would use it as a weapon if they got any closer. They were almost within arm's reach.

"We're not going to hurt you, much," the other man said. His accent made him difficult to understand, but Carly caught the meaning of his words. Their intentions weren't good. The thought of being anywhere near these two caused her to step back.

She accidentally tapped the red car with her behind. An alarm sounded and panic set in. Her heart raced as she swung the brush out in front of her. It wasn't necessary. The loud noise scared the men away. She overheard them curse as she breathed a sigh of relief, watching their coats disappear into the blizzard.

A close call. Whoever owned the car had unknowingly saved her. If they were close by, she would have kissed them and thanked them a million times over.

She leaned against her truck to catch her breath.

This day couldn't get any worse. The noise blared in her ear as she wiped the snow off her bottom. She turned her attention to the car, inspecting the flashy scrap of red metal for any damages. No dent, thank goodness.

The snow fell in sticky, wet clumps, soaking her hair and face. Her ears rang, and she wondered how such a little car could make so much noise. Soon the entire dinner would come out to investigate her small indiscretion. On cue, the owner of the sports car clicked a remote button, silencing the alarm.

"For your information, there's nothing worth stealing in there," Theo Montagne said, approaching the car. His dark blue eyes focused on her and this time her knees buckled a little. Of course, the car belonged to him. He lifted his hat, revealing more of his handsome face, like he wanted her to know who she was dealing with.

Carly's cheeks flushed a rosy color that had nothing to do with the cold weather. "I wasn't trying to steal anything. You parked way too close." Her initial reaction to smother the owner in kisses and thankyous wasn't going to happen.

"You're saying it's my fault you hit my car?" He closed the distance between them until he stood right next to her. She could feel his warm breath against her cheek and once again her knees buckled. She expected him to check out his car, but he kept his intense blues on her. His cocky grin sent goosebumps across her skin. If her heart hadn't already been racing, it would have started.

The air felt supercharged, like she was standing in an electrical vortex. "Um, I don't think the situation merits any blame. Your car alarm must be sensitive since I barely tapped it."

"So, you admit that you did hit my car." His tone was playful as he leaned against his hood like he had all the time in the world. A luxury she did not share.

Carly didn't have time for games, even if those games were with the super-hot and famous hockey player. She had a plane to catch and flirting with Theo Montagne wasn't on her to do list. First, he ignored her, and now he was being cute.

"There's no damage, look for yourself." She pointed to where she grazed his car, but his eyes went to her lips instead.

He licked over a small scar on his plump lower lip as he reached into his pocket and pulled out his phone. "You may have dented the door. I can't tell with all this snow. We should exchange contact information just in case I find some damage later on. Add your details."

She stepped away from his outstretched hand and wiped the heavy snow off her windshield with the brush again. "I bumped your car with my butt, there's no dent, and there's no way I'm giving you my information."

"Choosing the hard way, I dig it. Let's start with your name, sweetheart?"

Carly felt his eyes follow her rear as she finished clearing her windshield. She may have bent over more than required. When she looked back he was checking her out like it was the most natural and casual thing in the world. Most women probably fell at his feet, but she wouldn't be one of them. Her blood boiled at his arrogance. Her encounter with the two men was all but forgotten with him standing so close to her.

"My name is Carly Saint, and I am not your

sweetheart. Jackass." She used the brush to push the last of the snow towards him, covering his chin and jacket with snow. She laughed at the look of shock on his handsome face.

A smile curled at the corners of his mouth, finally he looked like a young twenty-year-old man. He shook out his jacket and laughed right along with her. A rich and profound sounding vibrato that enticed her senses. If she had more time, she might have stayed to hear more of that laugh, but she couldn't, moreover she shouldn't.

"You don't talk like a saint, but you look like an angel."

The compliment warmed her, but she knew better than to fall for smooth lines. Rather than go close to him again, she rounded the front of her truck to get away. She opened her passenger door and slid across to the driver's side.

Her attempt at a speedy getaway was foiled when her truck refused to start. The early nineties pickup struggled to turn over as she cranked the ignition. It hated the cold more than she did. She tried again and the old pile of crap showed no signs of life. Mr. Hockey-Heartthrob sat on the hood of his car with a bright big smile, watching her struggle.

Click, click, click. Nothing.

He was beginning to resemble a snowman as she kept trying and failing. She gave up, knowing the beast wouldn't cooperate. This wasn't the first time the truck had let her down. A look in the rearview mirror reflected a tired raccoon with big brown eyes. Hair clung to her face since the elastic no longer contained her auburn tendrils. She fixed her ponytail and wiped away the mascara from under her eyes. All the extra effort that morning was not reflected back.

With her tail between her legs, so to speak, she opened her door. This was so not how today was supposed to go. Carly searched the parking lot for options.

"Need a lift, Carly?" He asked as she closed the truck door behind her. "Or maybe you're hoping those big guys from the diner will come pick you up?" His joke wasn't funny.

A few cars down, she spotted a big white pickup truck idling. She couldn't be sure, but she assumed there were two men sitting inside. It was difficult to make out any faces from the distance, but she felt certain the occupants were the same men from earlier. They downright frightened her.

She wondered why they were still there with their truck running. It couldn't be them, surely, they had better things to do on Christmas Eve than scare the shit out of a waitress. Through the snow, she couldn't see anything but her gut told her they were staring at her. She shivered and wrapped her arms around her waist.

"Yes, I'll take a ride please," she said, turning her attention back to her knight in snowy armor. Her rush to leave had doubled in the last few minutes.

He came around his car and opened the passenger door for her like an old-fashioned gentleman. Carly slid into the warmth and his manly scent made her forget all about the truck and the strange men lingering outside her work. The heat from the seats and the air was a welcomed reprieve from the cold.

The hockey players big body settled into the tiny driver's seat, his arm touching hers. "I'm Theo, by the way. So, where are we headed?"

"Away from here," she said. The sooner the better.

CHAPTER FOUR

The storm struck them with its fury once they hit the highway. Carly leaned forward and gripped the dashboard, struggling to see the lines or any bare concrete through the wall of white. The windshield wipers failed to keep up with the onslaught from Mother Nature.

Theo hadn't balked when she asked him to take her to the airport. Turned out he was heading there as well, both of them traveling home for the holidays. After the initial few words, the conversation dropped to a standstill as they both attempted to see the road before them.

Curiosity sat like a devil on her shoulder, demanding she ask the hockey-legend-in-the-making why he was at her diner. He seemed larger than life on TV, and his disarming smile continued that impression. The truck stop diner wasn't a place she expected someone like him to frequent. She wasn't sure if she should ask. Regardless of his reason for

C

being there, she was glad to be getting a ride.

"It doesn't look pretty out there." Theo smiled and all thoughts or questions evaporated.

That smile was a lethal weapon that slaughtered her defenses. She didn't want to be attracted to him, but only a superhuman could resist. At eighteen she hadn't fine-tuned those skills yet. He radiated an animal magnetism or pheromones she was powerless against.

A ride to the airport was all he offered, however another kind of ride came to mind. She pictured them in the back seat, his face confined between her thighs as he pressed his full lips against her heated flesh. His tongue sliding through her wet folds until he found the part of her that begged to be licked. She imagined herself, hands planted on the ceiling, her knees on the soft leather, and screaming his name as he devoured her.

Carly shifted in her seat and pressed her knees together. Something like that would never happen. From that point on, it was easier to concentrate on the road. Every time Carly glanced at Theo she'd get heated all over again and her mind would come up with another naughty scenario. All of them involved him naked and her coming.

Being trapped in a confined space with Theo wasn't good for her psyche. She needed to get out of the car and pull her mind out of the gutter. Having a crush on a hockey player was a bad idea. The worst idea ever.

Time moved fast, but the miles did not. The drive should have taken less than an hour, but it looked like it might take three or more at the speed they traveled. There was no way she was making her early evening flight. She wondered if they would even make it to the city at all.

Theo concentrated on the road and didn't fill the silence with chitchat which Carly appreciated. She worried his smooth voice would only make her more turned on, like adding fuel to a fire that was already burning out of control. He turned up the stereo and let the beats do the talking. The techno bass was a welcome distraction from the non-stop carols. The car hydroplaned more than once before he broke the silence with a loud sigh.

"I'm sorry, but the airport won't happen tonight. This isn't safe. I can't see the pavement or the lines anymore. We have to turn back."

She hated to admit defeat, but in this case, it was the safest option. "The flights are probably canceled now, anyway. It's better to be safe than sorry." Carly twisted her fingers in her lap. "Thanks for trying, Theo."

The thought of spending Christmas alone in her dorm made her want to cry. She could ask her boss to join him and his family, but it wouldn't be the same. Her eyes filled with tears she refused to let fall. Theo must have caught her blinking away the moisture because his large hand covered hers for a moment. The warmth spread over her like a blanket, but too soon he took it away.

"Don't be sad. We'll figure something out. Do you live near the diner?"

Men hated it when women cried, at least in Carly's experience. She guessed Theo was more like everyone else. Too much emotion made him uncomfortable.

"No," she replied, annoyed at herself for getting

upset and at him for being such a guy.

"I know I'm not family, but we can make the best of the situation. Are you worried we'll crash, cause I'm an awesome driver. I promise I'll keep you safe." Theo's words were comforting, but came across as overly optimistic.

Every interview she'd seen Theo give, he radiated positivity. He never said an unkind word and somehow found the positives even after a loss. Carly considered herself a realist, and this Christmas looked bleak.

"My place is on the south side of the city, taking that option out. So where do you live?" He asked after another few minutes of silence.

"I'm south as well, I live on campus; U of M."

He whistled. "That's nowhere near here. Why do you work so far?"

"The owners remind me of my parents, and we have a similar diner back home. Small town roots and all that."

Theo glanced her way quickly. "I take that to mean your folks don't live in the area?"

It was sweet he was curious about her, but the thought of her parents spending Christmas alone made her sad all over again. They were bound to be disappointed and heartbroken by her absence.

"Neither of us is from the area. No big deal, we'll salvage this Christmas once we're back at the diner," he said when she didn't respond.

"We?" She turned in her seat to face him.

His smile spread from ear to ear. "Yeah, we're in this together, sweetheart." He winked, and Carly couldn't help but giggle at his cockiness. "That's a beautiful sound. Laugh in the face of adversity."

"You are something else," she said.

He shrugged his shoulders before responding. "That's a good thing, right?" Theo reduced their speed to a near crawl. The hazard lights didn't help the visibility, there could be other cars on the road and they wouldn't know. Carly didn't notice the off-ramp sign, and they missed the first chance to turn around.

The slow pace didn't stop the car from sliding on the sheet of ice that was once pavement. Carly felt the car slipping on the ice more than once, but Theo kept them out of the ditch. "I'm not sure we'll even make it back there. We might be better to find a place to ride out this storm." She wasn't a fan of her own suggestion.

Theo gripped the steering wheel tight. His knuckles turned white as he attempted to keep them on the road. "You're the boss."

A moment later Carly's stomach jumped into her throat as the car spun out of control. The three-hundred-sixty-degree turn stole the air from her lungs. Her nails dug into his thigh. Life did not flash before her eyes, and she didn't have any kind of epiphany. All Carly thought of in that split second was how upset her parents would be if she didn't survive.

Theo kept the car from spinning off the road, but for how much longer Carly wondered. They needed to get off the roads until the blizzard passed. Her mind raced into the ditch where the red death trap almost took them. Theo had a bright future ahead of him and tons of people who depended on him. Carly's future wasn't so cheery, but it was hers, and she wasn't ready to die.

"That was a close call." He patted her hand, which was still glued to his leg. "You okay?"

Her pulse raced like she'd completed the hundred-meter dash, and she struggled to catch her next breath. No part of their predicament was okay. Driving in these conditions was stupid and could get them killed. Any hope of having a happy holiday was gone, but she kept all those thoughts to herself. "I'm fine, you?"

She noticed how solid his leg felt under her hand. A hand that was precariously close to his crotch. Her eyes drifted down to his lap and her pinky finger rested against the thick bulge. He must have felt her, but didn't mind because he didn't push her away. Her finger inadvertently twitched along the side of his cock. Oh Lord, she touched Theo Montagne's penis. Carly blushed, embarrassed by the reflex and withdrew her hand.

He didn't say a word, simply nodded and drove at a snail's pace all over again. She kept her eyes off Theo and kept her hands to herself from that moment on. They didn't miss the next exit. The conditions weren't much better off the highway, but they stayed on the road.

"We'll take the first road we see and hope that some nice people lets us in."

His plan sounded good. The first road was a gravel one which led them for miles before the first building appeared. Carly shook her head when the small farm house came into view. It looked old and empty, but it also looked safer than braving the roads for another minute.

"Come on, let's check if anyone is home." Theo unbuckled his seat belt.

The skies darkened with the late afternoon hour. Her phone had no service, meaning there was no one coming to help. Theo whipped around the car and opened her door, surprising Carly with his chivalry. The wind had picked up since leaving work. Carly lifted the hood on her red jacket to cover her ears. She looked into the backseat and realized she'd forgotten her bags.

"Dammit!" She mumbled under the breath.

"What's wrong?" He asked, placing his hand against her back.

She could have stepped away but didn't. "I forgot my luggage in my truck." Carly looked up and caught his sly grin.

It was obvious he had his own ideas why that happened. He probably thought she was so taken by his awesomeness that she forgot her stuff. The truth was she'd been so scared; she hadn't thought of anything except getting away from the terrifying men. That was not something she planned to tell Theo.

"I'll leave mine in the car for now. Let's get out of the snow." Theo tucked her body close to his as they hurried towards the run-down two-story house. Being so close felt natural, too comfortable.

No lights were on and she got the impression that nobody would be home. She knocked and listened for a response that never came. Theo tried the door, but it was locked. They both knocked several times and called out into the blizzard, but no one answered.

They didn't have many options since driving was out of the question. Carly looked back towards the car located only steps away and she could barely make it out. They could hunker down inside, but they didn't have enough fuel to keep it running for too much longer.

"Stay here; I will run around back and see if I can find a way inside." Theo tried the handle again without success.

Her eyes widened at his suggestion. "We can't break in. It's against the law." She placed her body against the door, creating a human barricade. Carly planned on becoming a top-notch scientist. She hoped to win a Nobel prize at some point in her career, and a criminal record would eliminate that possibility.

"We can't stay out here and freeze to death either. It's survival 101: seek shelter." He pinched the tip of her nose, then bounded down the side of the house and disappeared into the storm.

Her pity party kicked into full force. First, she had to work on Christmas Eve, which was already bad enough without the rest of her crap day piled on top. She hadn't made great tips, considering the season, plus she'd encountered those strange and scary men. At least Theo's car had scared them off, but if she caused any damage, she had no means to pay for the repairs. Add that she missed her flight home, and now she was stranded in the middle of nowhere. The only silver lining she found was Theo.

He showed up at the right time and so far, he'd proven to be a decent guy. Things could have been way worse if she'd been driving her truck alone. She might not have made it safely to this house. A rattling sound came from inside seconds before the door opened. She stumbled backwards taken by surprise.

Theo caught her before she fell on her butt and chuckled as she straightened up. He pulled her inside and closed the door. "Sorry, I thought you heard me yell once I made it in."

She wiped the snow off her coat with her hands. Some of the larger clumps landed on Theo, but he didn't notice or care. "Clearly, I didn't. And for the record, I'm not okay with breaking and entering." She gave him a stern look, which only increased the size of his smile. A heart-stopping, panty-dropping smile.

"I'm a law-abiding citizen, the back door was unlocked." He held his hands up in surrender. "Swear. We're alone." His blue eyes twinkled with mischief.

Her breath hitched. The reality set in; she was alone with Theo Montagne. Drops of water fell from his hair and ran down his face. He turned the lights on, and Carly saw more of his handsome features. His jaw had that ultra-sexy five o'clock shadow thing happening. The feel of those prickly whiskers against her cheek, or better yet her thighs would drive her wild.

This was so not the time to get all gooey-eyed over him. She had to focus on something other than the two of them being alone. "I'm not sure how I can thank you properly for getting us here safe and sound, except to say thank you. But—"

"You can pay me with kisses if you want?" He puckered his full lips and made a kissing sound. His actions infuriated her as much as they caused her pulse to race. Cocky bastard.

Not everyone wanted to kiss him, did they?

Carly looked away, unable to take him seriously. The adrenaline of the near-death drive here was making him talk crazy, or the man was an incurable flirt. She suspected the latter to be true. The fact that she wouldn't mind his form of payment meant that the storm, coupled with being in an enclosed car with Theo, had officially messed with her brain.

She closed her eyes and counted backwards from fifty to calm herself. A trick she'd learned as a kid to deal with her anxiety. She hoped it would do the same to calm her raging hormones. This was new territory.

No matter how appealing his lips might be, they shouldn't trespass. She took a deep breath and exhaled slowly. "We have to go."

She opened her eyes and Theo was nowhere to be seen.

CHAPTER FIVE

She had to convince him this was a horrible idea.
The question was how could she make him
understand when the reasons had little to do with the
house or storm, and everything to do with him.

In the corner of the room, she spotted a fake
Christmas tree decorated with blue and white ribbons,
but there were no presents underneath. It seemed like
a masculine tree and the rest of the furnishings
matched her theory. This house lacked a woman's
touch. But the family portrait on the wall showed a
couple and a young teenage daughter.

The old house and picture reminded her of her
own family. They always cut down a real tree, and the
base overflowed with gifts. Carly was spoiled in many
ways, but never the way she wanted. The festivities
would go on without her this year, and she hated the
thought of intruding and interrupting another family's
special day.

They couldn't stay; Theo would have to

understand.

The house didn't have an open layout like most modern homes, but it didn't take long to find him. She opened the door to the kitchen and found Theo looking through the cabinets. The dark jeans hugged his perfectly round butt as he bent to check a lower drawer. The urge to walk over and grab a handful was too much. She admired the view for a moment longer than she should have.

"What are you doing?" Her voice had a groggy, almost breathless tone she didn't recognize. She cleared her throat.

He didn't turn around. "Checking for supplies. We might be snowed in for a day or two. It's pretty bad out there, in case you didn't realize."

An overnight with Theo would test her resolve to be alone. The more time she spent with him the dirtier her thoughts became. Too much time with him, and there was no telling what she'd end up saying or doing. She couldn't let him know she was attracted to him because his ego didn't need padding but her heart did.

Carly rolled her eyes. "I noticed. I don't think we should steal from these people. It's bad enough we're in their home uninvited."

Theo reached into his back pocket and pulled out his wallet. "We're not stealing. I will pay for anything we use and leave them a thank you note." He tossed some bills on the wooden kitchen table. "I'm not throwing a party and trashing the place. Lighten up."

He needed to get serious. "We can't stay. I'm not comfortable being in here. As I was saying earlier, I appreciate you bringing us here safely, I really do. But we need to move along and find another house."

Theo straightened his posture and put his hands on his hips. "What's got you spooked?"

"I'm not scared!" She mimicked his stance.

He smiled at her response. "Tell me; are you uncomfortable because the home owners aren't here to invite us in with open arms, or is it the fact that you're alone with me?"

His arrogance astounded her. "Let me set the record straight for you, Mr. I'm-Way-Too-Cocky, I am not in any way scared of being alone with you, because nothing will happen."

He stepped towards her and she held her ground. "Are you sure you don't want something to happen?" He arched a brow, looking at her like a man starving for a kiss. Or maybe that was her look reflected within his cerulean swirls.

Why did he have to be so tempting?

If he was an ordinary man, Carly suspected she would have kissed him right then and there. Thrown caution to the wind and ended her dry spell. But he wasn't just a hockey player, he was Theo Montagne. A very well-known player. Carly wouldn't let herself forget that fact.

"Positive." She licked her lips. "Now, I will repeat myself since you seem to be hard of hearing. We need to leave." Carly turned towards the door to break the heated connection that left her stomach in knots and her heart pounding in her ears.

He placed his hand on the small of her back. "If you insist, then after you."

She expected more of a fight. He was enjoying her discomfort far too much, and his hand felt too warm against the patch of bare skin between her shirt and jeans. The heat spread through her until her toes felt hot.

"Great, I'm sure we can find a house that doesn't require any felony charges."

"Whatever you say, Carly." The way he said her name sent goosebumps to explode across her skin.

They walked to the entry and put their jackets and boots back on. Theo's cocky smile never wavered, like he was privy to a secret she had yet to discover. She didn't care for that smile. She asked him to go back as he had entered, and lock the front door. He left her there on the steps.

The snow somehow came down even worse than before if that was possible. Their footsteps from earlier had been covered, leaving no trail towards the vehicle. Carly could barely make out the car which wasn't more than a few feet away. There were no other houses nearby, at least none she saw. She second guessed her request to leave and questioned her own motives.

Theo had called her bluff in the kitchen, being alone with him made her nervous. She admitted she was far more attracted to him than she would have liked. He made it too easy with his suggestive smiles and easy-going attitude.

She slogged through the snow and waited for him by the car. He didn't make her wait long.

"Your chariot awaits," he said, opening the passenger door.

She got in and watched as he attempted to wipe the snow off the car before getting in. "It's miserable out there. Is it me, or does it seem worse?"

"It's not you. I'm not making any promises about what we'll find next. We can't drive around looking for a house full of people. Even if there's no one at the next house we're staying there. Deal?"

She did not want to be alone with him, but she had little to bargain with. "Deal."

The tires spun, but the car didn't move when Theo put it into drive. He pressed on the gas and Carly heard the engine roar as the tires found traction and lurched forward. She couldn't make out the driveway, let alone the turn to get onto the road ahead. Theo's gesture to humor her irrational request would end with them hurt or dead. She couldn't let that happen.

"Stop." They hadn't made it over ten feet.

Theo stopped the car. "What's wrong?"

"We aren't going to make it to another house in this. The storm has sealed our fate and whoever lives here; odds are they won't be coming home until the weather breaks. I was wrong to ask you to drive us out of here. I'm sorry."

"Wow, a woman who admits to being wrong. Will you marry me?" He smiled and diffused the somber mood she had created for herself.

She slapped his arm playfully. "No, and I figured if we can't make it out of here, then the cops can't get here to arrest us."

Theo laughed, and the sound sent butterflies dancing through her belly. "Can't disagree with your logic." He put the car in park and killed the engine. "Wait here a moment, I'll run around back and come back to get you. There's no sense in your waiting in the snow."

"That's okay, I can go back with you." She didn't want him going out of his way. He'd already done enough by taking her to safety.

He opened her car door and held onto her hand

once she was out. The gesture was caring and didn't make her uncomfortable. It meant nothing, he was being kind, she told herself. She was thankful for his quick hands when she slipped halfway around the car. His strong arms caught her, pressing her body against his. The snow covered them both and as she looked up into his face her breath seized. He was magnificent. If he leaned down and kissed her, she would have let him.

His eyes found hers and for a moment, she thought he might. Then he blinked, the blizzard spell broken, and he took a step back. There was no kiss, and she berated herself for even thinking there might be. He was a flirt, nothing more. She attempted to convince herself he wasn't her type. Although, she would wager Theo Montagne was everyone's type.

Once back inside, they returned to the kitchen. That seemed like a safe place to be together.

"Are you feeling more comfortable about being here now?" He asked as he opened a cabinet containing pots and pans.

"I'm okay," she said with a smile. "Think they have any chocolate?" If he could make the best of this situation, then so could she. She walked passed him and opened the pantry. There were plenty of canned and dry goods available. She looked over her shoulder after a moment.

He raised a brow. "Okay," he repeated. "Didn't see any chocolate but I'm hungry. How about you?"

"I could eat." Carly looked out the large kitchen window at the endless waterfall of white. "Since you drove us here, it's only fair I make dinner. We might lose power soon, so we'll need flashlights and candles."

"Good call; I'm on it." Theo checked the drawers but came up empty.

"Don't snoop on these people. Check the hall closets, but the less we disrupt the better. Got it?"

He nodded and left to search for supplies. Carly gathered what she needed to prepare a quick meal and got busy cooking. Nothing fancy, some fried ham, macaroni and cheese with a side of canned green beans. It should satisfy their hunger and not put out the owners in any way.

She was plating their meal when Theo returned, holding a handful of candles. Carly prayed they wouldn't need them. Karma laughed in her face when a moment later, the lights went out.

CHAPTER SIX

Theo walked over to the table. "Guess we'll be eating by candlelight," he said, lighting the first set of candles.

The flames licked across his features like a soft caress. Carly had always wanted to have a romantic candlelight dinner, but the occasion had never come up. Until now. This was so not going to help her resolve to stay away from all hockey players, including Theo. "I guess so."

The round wooden kitchen table was set for two, with a red linen tablecloth and three small votive candles. Carly sat across from Theo as they ate by candle light. She always dreamed one day she'd meet a man who would love her unconditionally, share romantic dinners and read her poetry. The man of her dreams was fictitious, he didn't exist.

"Thanks for making dinner," he said between bites.

Carly couldn't help but compare him to the men

of her past. In the looks department, he outshone the others by a landslide. Her exes were similar in build and attractive in their own ways, but not drool worthy like Mr. Montagne.

Her two high school boyfriends had been jocks. They didn't understand the first thing about romance. Too young, selfish and self-centered to think of putting in any effort. It took Carly way too long to realize she deserved better. To an athlete, the sport always came first. A lesson she wouldn't forget.

"You're welcome." Her gaze followed the light as it flickered against Theo.

The soft glow of the flames sent shadows dancing across the room. Somehow it softened the hard lines of Theo's face, making him appear even more handsome and flawless. The entire time they were eating, Theo's eyes stayed locked on hers. A battle of blue versus brown.

She wondered what he saw when he looked at her? Did he see the wholesome country girl Miranda claimed she was, or did he see the tomboy her father saw? Whatever it was, he seemed to like looking.

Watching him devour his meal was highly erotic. He licked his fork, and the tines slid across the small scar on his lip, making her clench her thighs. She couldn't stop memorizing every one of his features and imagining what they felt like.

They ate in relative silence, each of them wrapped up in their own world. Theo checked off all of her attraction boxes. Tall, solid build and a smile that could make her do just about anything. She had to watch out for smiles like his. They had gotten her into trouble before, and she vowed never to repeat her past mistakes. Yet, when he hummed his satisfaction at the end of their meal, and gifted her with a genuinely satisfied smile, she nearly came undone.

Carly would never look at mac and cheese the same way again.

Theo offered to clear their plates and clean up. She didn't protest because she had to get away. The room was far too sexually charged. She feared if she helped him wash up, she might throw him against the wall and bite the scar she'd stared at all throughout dinner.

Carly retreated to the couch next to the Christmas tree to take stock of her situation. These feelings were all wrong. Theo Montagne was Mr. Hockey-Player. A player. She got the distinct impression he liked her as in wanted to sleep with her. The bedroom eyes he sent her way weren't in her imagination.

Her roommate would hate her if she hooked up with someone from the potential husband list. The kind of men Carly deemed as inappropriate dating material. She wasn't wrong, but none of those reasons could stop the overwhelming urge to kiss him. Those indecent thoughts had to go. She would not kiss Theo. The storm cut the power to the house and her brain. Her libido was on the verge of short circuiting.

The brown upholstered couch was more comfortable than Carly expected. After lighting two candles on the coffee table, she curled into a ball and sank further into the cushions. She tried not to think about Theo and the sweet way he pulled out her chair at dinner, or how he anticipated her needs. The way he was taking care of her, not because he had to, but because he chose to.

"All clean," Theo said as he plopped down next to her. His leg touched hers and she shivered. "Are you cold? I found some blankets earlier in the closet where I grabbed the candles and flashlights. I brought them out here."

The arrogance from inside the diner, and the bravado he displayed in the parking lot, was replaced with an allure she found difficult to ignore. She wondered if this charming Theo was the real him, or if the usual too-cool jock personality, she knew all too well would make an ugly appearance.

Carly shook her head, knowing the gooseflesh had nothing to do with the temperature. "I'm fine." She avoided eye contact and stared out the large picture window. There wasn't much to see outside besides a white horizontal wave of snow against the darkness of night.

"Is that code for you are ticked off at me? My ex used to say fine all the time whenever I did something she didn't like." Theo stretched his long legs and planted them between the candles on the table. His green socks had tiny candy canes all over them. They matched her red socks with the same design.

Carly laughed. "Nice socks." She kicked out one foot from under her and wiggled her toes in his direction.

Theo grabbed her ankle and inspected the Christmas sock. "Did you pick yours out or were they a gift?" He didn't release her foot, instead he settled it on his lap and kneaded her insole.

It felt like heaven, transporting her to a place of coveted bliss. "I bought them, and you don't have to massage my feet." He pressed hard against a tight spot and Carly moaned. "On second thought, don't stop." She changed positions, placing her other foot on his lap.

"Appears we have something in common."

Carly reached over, grabbed a throw cushion and smacked him with it. "Is that a dig because I'm not a popular superstar athlete like you?"

Theo laughed as he stole the pillow and placed it under his head. "Not everyone loves Christmas, but it is my favorite time of year. Before you say anything, it's not about the presents. Don't get me wrong, I like gifts, but it's all about family and giving. My mom always made a big production. Does your family go overboard?" He went back to massaging her foot, applying the perfect amount of pressure to make her swoon.

"I'm an only child, so my parents spoiled me. This is our first Christmas apart and I don't think they will handle it well. They kind of hate me going to school so far away. How about you, I bet your family will miss having you home?"

Theo got quiet, and she thought he hadn't heard her. He continued to massage her feet and she soaked in the soothing sensations. A few minutes passed, Carly almost fell asleep before he answered. "My mom passed away a few years back."

He said nothing more for a while. Carly didn't know what to say, so she stayed quiet.

"It's just my dad and my two older brothers now. Hockey comes first, so they weren't expecting me home for the holidays." He sighed heavily. "To be honest with you, we haven't celebrated since she died. It's a shame because she would be pissed to see what our family has become without her." A wistful look ghosted across his features but was soon replaced with a sad smile. "This tree over here is nice, don't you think?"

"Kind of manly, but it is nice." Carly wasn't expecting him to have a less than perfect home life. He acted larger than life and always had a smile for the cameras.

"I'm sorry about your mom." She leaned over and covered his hand with hers. His hands stilled. "I can tell you miss her. I'm not sure what I would do if my mom wasn't around when I needed her." Carly dreaded even the thought of her parents not being a phone call away. They were close. The urge to reach out to them and tell them she was okay gnawed at her. They must be worried sick by now.

"I do, miss her I mean. She was so full of life and smiles. She never got too serious, about hockey or anything in life, which is something I try to copy. It's hard, because she made it seem easy." He rubbed her feet again.

Carly leaned back into the couch. "You're succeeding then, because I've only ever seen you with a smile, except for today. On the ice you're a fierce competitor, but off it, you seem like a happy guy. I figured you for a guy who didn't have a care in the world."

Theo shrugged his shoulders. "You said something earlier too, so, you know who I am. Does that mean you're a hockey enthusiast or are you a Theo Montagne admirer?" His smile broadened, and a dimple emerged to torment her.

"I may be a fan of your team," she answered.

He tickled instead of rubbing and Carly squealed. "Did you hit my car on purpose to get my attention? You wouldn't be the first you know."

Again, with the arrogance. Carly rolled her eyes as she tried to pull her tortured tootsies away from his strong hold but it was in vain. She thought back to the two men from the diner, and the one with the gross-looking scratches in particular. It gave her the creeps all over again. "No, I wasn't trying to get your attention. Get over yourself, hockey star."

"You've called me that a few times now, what's with that?"

Her roommate wasn't the only one who enjoyed watching hockey. Unlike her friend, Carly enjoyed the sport not the men. She rebuffed all men, but provided an extra cold shoulder to the hockey players. That didn't mean she didn't love watching the games. "I may have caught more than a few of your games," she admitted.

In that moment, she was afraid what else she might admit. Like the fact that she liked Theo, way more than she intended to. She knew if she didn't move away from him soon, her feet wouldn't be the only thing in his lap.

She wasn't ready to go there. No matter how much of a good guy he seemed, he was still a player. She pulled her feet off his legs, planted them on the floor, and walked over to the window. The storm had to end and it couldn't come soon enough for Carly.

"I don't like hockey players." The statement burst from her lips before she could take it back. "Let me rephrase; I don't like hockey players as boyfriends."

He stood beside her and pulled her chin towards him. "I can understand that, we're a difficult group to love." His eyes moved from hers and he looked out the window.

Whoa, she never mentioned love. "I'm sure you're a great person and any woman would be lucky to fall in love with you."

His eyes were so blue, she was drowning within their waters while he peeked into her soul. As though he knew her defenses were weakening with every moment she was with him. She wasn't aware of her movement, but she leaned towards him. He leaned in close as well and this was the moment she'd been dreading and hoping for, since she noticed him walk into the diner. This kiss would change everything.

CHAPTER SEVEN

His breath fluttered against her lips. The warm wet invitation was almost too appealing to turn down, but she pulled away.

All of her previous mistakes flashed before her. She wasn't interested in being a hockey player's hookup or anything else. Theo more than likely had millions of girls throwing themselves at him, and she would not be one of them.

"What's wrong?" Theo asked as she put some distance between them.

She walked only a few feet away to stand by the tree. The glass ornaments cast an eerie vibe to the branches, and the room felt like it was closing in on her. There was no misinterpretation. Theo was going to kiss her. Another second and their mouths would have connected. A kiss that wouldn't have ended there.

So many possibilities.

That was the problem because there was only

one possible outcome from that kiss. Sex complicated everything and Carly wasn't looking for another notch on her bedpost. Another man to skate over her, leaving his marks behind.

The mixed signals were her fault. As much as she didn't want to open herself to him, she owed him an explanation. Rip off the Band-Aid, she told herself. The sooner she laid the ground rules the better off they would both be. So why was she hesitating?

"I told you I don't kiss hockey players, and you are most definitely a hockey player."

He laughed and walked in the opposite direction shielding his face. "I've never been turned down because of my job before. That's a new one, and pretty shallow." He called her shallow.

"Pardon me?"

"You heard me. I think that it's extremely judgmental to stereotype me based on my job. My work doesn't define who I am, any more than your choice of schools defines you."

Exhausted from the barrage of emotions, she wasn't sure what to say. Carly slid her fingertips over the silk ribbon on the tree, admiring the way it contrasted against the fake bristles of the evergreen.

Theo had some valid points. She never thought of it along those lines, but she wasn't superficial. Athletes, regardless of their sport, were bad news, and she had her reasons to stay away.

"Doesn't matter what you think. I won't get involved with anyone who plays sports. No offense to you, it's not personal, it's my choice."

He came up behind her. His heat radiated against her back. "I do take offense. Won't you give me a chance?"

"No." She turned, and he stood inches from her, holding a piece of mistletoe above her head. "What are you doing?"

"Making sure I get a chance."

His lips covered hers with the right amount of pressure to make her pulse race. She opened her mouth to him and he took full advantage. Their tongues wrapped around one another in a blissful encounter. All the joy of being a kid opening a present, tearing through the wrapping paper to find your new favorite toy, that's what it was like kissing Theo. Carly's head spun and her toes curled. Theo kissed with purpose and with the same skill she'd seen him display on the ice.

The softest pillow-like lips molded against hers. The velvet smoothness of his tongue encircled around hers. She was making out with Theo Montagne. She'd kissed others before, but none displayed the amount of skill Theo possessed.

His hand moved to her hip, and the cold of his fingertips brushed against her stomach.

"We should stop," she said as he licked down the column of her throat.

"I couldn't disagree more."

He kissed her again, with renewed vigor. She could feel his determination to change her mind. As if a kiss could prove they were perfect for one another. As though this one moment could erase years of pain. When their lips were sealed together, nothing else mattered, she got lost in the sensations. He growled when she latched onto the scar on his lip and sucked it into her mouth. He tasted better than she imagined.

She hadn't noticed they were moving until the back of her knees hit the couch and she fell backwards onto it. His mouth never left hers. He was so strong and so good at this. Too good. She placed her hands against the solid muscles of his chest.

"I can't do this with you," she said, pushing him off her. They both moved to their respective corners of the couch. "I'm sorry.

"I'm not. That was amazing and I know you feel whatever it is between us too. If you need time, I'm a patient man."

"Theo… I, we—"

"Okay, Miss Smarty-Pants, why don't we share secrets and get to know each other better." Theo cocked his head to the side and flashed her a cocky grin. His charms wouldn't get him anywhere with her.

She crossed her arms over her chest. She was not in the mood for games and shook her head from side to side in silent refusal.

"Come on, we've got time to kill. Would it make you more comfortable if I went first?" He asked, sitting upright on the couch next to her. It didn't escape her notice he had moved closer. His arm grazed her leg and shivers raced across her covered skin.

Every time they touched she reacted the same. Would that ever stop?

Theo exuded some serious heat as Carly shifted away from him. She was already too warm. "No, thank you. I don't want to know your deepest, darkest secrets and I most certainly do not care to share mine."

She kept her eyes on the window because she couldn't do anything else. Spilling her guts to the hockey superstar made her want to run back outside barefoot until the skies cleared. Plus, if she looked at

Theo she would have to admit that up close he might be the best-looking man she had ever seen. He wasn't perfect, which made him more attractive. The tiny delicious scar on his lip was one of many, no doubt received from sticks and pucks to the face.

From the corner of her eye, she caught Theo sink back into the worn cushions. He placed his feet on the coffee table without a care in the world. "All right, I'll go first," he said, ignoring her refusal to play along. Theo linked his fingers behind his head, appearing relaxed and at ease. The opposite of her at that moment.

Carly huffed an exasperated breath, this guy couldn't take anything serious. "Why do we need to get to know each other? Can't we sit here quietly and wait out the storm?"

"I like your feistiness, are you this way around all men, or is this snarky attitude reserved for me?"

Carly turned and glared at him. Theo got under her skin when he shouldn't. Why did being alone with him put her on edge? He's just a boy, like all the others, she reminded herself. No one special. Right, who was she kidding. Instead of ripping into him she closed her eyes and counted backwards from fifty. Her angst wasn't with him, it was with herself.

"What are you doing? Are you counting?"

Carly finished her comforting ritual before responding. "Yes, I count as a way of calming myself. I'm sorry for being rude with you, it's this situation." She opened her eyes and found him leaning forward, mere inches from her face. His eyes fastened onto her lips. "I mean, this... this isn't how I expected to spend Christmas."

"This might be my favorite Christmas ever." He

shifted himself closer, his leg next to hers. "It's not every day I get to spend my holidays with a beautiful woman."

Carly laughed. Was this guy for real? "Those lines might work on your many admirers, but I'm not falling for any of it. You didn't notice me when I was serving you coffee. I'm no more special now. The only reason you want to kiss me is because we're stuck here together and I'm saying no."

"Or… I want to kiss you, because you are exactly the girl I've been looking for. Strong, smart and sexy, sounds like a good package to me." Theo tucked a wayward curl behind her ear. His touch was soft and gentle. Carly would have moved away, but she was already pressed against the armrest.

"Trust me when I say I'm none of those things, except smart. I'm too smart to fall for cheesy pickup lines. Don't you have your fill of hockey bimbo's throwing themselves at you?"

His finger trailed down her cheek and cupped her jaw. "Did I mention sassy is at the top of my list? Carly, did I offend you by not falling at your feet in the restaurant?"

"No, I wouldn't expect that. But I know your type. You hockey players are all the same. The I'm here for a good-time not a long-time kind of guy. Am I right?"

"Wrong. Just so you know, I had one girlfriend throughout high school and still dated the same girl my first year after being drafted into the league. We broke up this past summer, and I have dated no one since her. It was a mutual decision since she didn't want to leave Montreal. We had been growing apart, and I was okay with her not coming west. She's moved on already, but I wasn't ready until recently. Carly, I'm not sure who you think I am, but I'm not a player."

This news forced Carly to admit she'd judged Theo prematurely. That could have been a lie, but she didn't think it was. Painting him with the same brush as the other hockey players wasn't fair. "I'm sorry. Beth, my roommate has dated a few of your teammates, and let's just say they weren't the best guys. They used her, and I don't want to get hurt."

"Some of my teammates like the attention the girls offer. The recognition and fame can go to your head. Especially the young guys my age. Puck bunnies are around every corner, it's a novelty some guys can't resist. But the majority are decent guys. Relationships end and people get hurt, but it's still worth the risk. If you ask me."

"Are you a decent guy, Theo?" Carly desperately wanted him to be a good guy. The world had enough bad boys.

"I try to be." He licked his lips again.

A lump formed in her throat as her walls crumbled. What if they kissed again, would that be so bad? "What are you looking for, Theo? Are you worth the risk?" Her voice sounded throaty and hoarse.

"You tell me." He inched closer until there was no distance between them.

The intensity in his eyes overwhelmed her. "Some risks might be worth taking." Carly was a planner, not a risk taker.

"You might be the perfect girl, Carly. Can I tell you a secret?" He took her hand and drew lazy circles on her palm.

The contact stole her sanity. Unable to say another word, she nodded in response.

"All I've ever wanted to do was play for the NHL. But with that job comes a lot of expectations. More demands than I ever thought possible, and that's just from my family. Everybody wants something from me, even my dad."

"Is that who you were chatting with at the diner?"

Theo looked away for a second and his intensity softened a little. "Yeah, he wants me home for the holidays but not for a family Christmas. It's mostly so him and my brothers can drill me about my performance thus far. Oh, besides the unsolicited coaching, he'll want to parade me around the legion. I've become a commodity."

"What do you want?" She asked, taking his face between her hands.

His blue eyes looked to hers for answers. Ones she couldn't provide. "I've been asking myself that a lot these days. In this business, it's hard to trust people. They tell you what they think you want to hear, but rarely ask what I want."

Carly smiled. This was their most honest conversation yet and things were getting real. Theo leaned in and pressed his lips against hers again. She melted into him, and she didn't have the strength to push him away.

CHAPTER EIGHT

His lips consumed hers, leaving no pretense behind. The scruff on his chin tickled. Theo kissed her with a finesse and skill mere mortals couldn't emulate. She liked the feel of his mouth on hers; of his cheek under her hands. She opened and granted him full access. He took advantage and Carly liquefied into a puddle of lust.

He moved their bodies into a lying position on the couch. His body covered hers, but he kept his weight to the side, propped on his elbows. The sensual way Theo kissed blew her Christmas print socks off. A mix of hard yet soft, demanding but inviting. Never had her tongue relished the taste of another.

Their lips were locked, and fused together by the laws of attraction. Too overwhelmed by the sensations coursing through her body, she couldn't stop. As the kiss grew more intense, so did her desire to touch him. Her fingers itched to feel more of him.

To learn and explore every inch of his body.

She dove her hands into the soft mop of his hair, twisting at the strands. He seemed to enjoy her playful side as he growled when she pulled harder, angling his head for a deeper kiss. She couldn't get enough.

His tongue licked along her bottom lip as he maneuvered her shirt up over her breasts. The kiss broke for a moment as his eyes devoured her body. His fingers worked the front clasp of her red bra. It popped open, freeing her breasts from their satin confines.

The color of his irises became the most breathtaking shade of cobalt as he ran the tip of his fingers over her nipple. It beaded under his gentle caress. He plucked at both tips, alternating and watching them harden. "You're beautiful," he said, as he palmed one breast in his large hand.

Carly believed him. She no longer had a reason to doubt his words.

It was only fair, if he got to look, then so should she. She tugged at the hem of his sweater and he pulled it off, tossing the garment to the floor. Theo Montagne was ripped. His body was in peak physical condition.

Carly reached for his thick biceps. He satisfied her arm fetish and then some. She could not wrap her hands around the muscle, but she didn't need to, to pull him on top of her. Skin to skin. Her breasts were crushed against a wall of solid muscles, and she liked it. This time, she kissed him and it was the most intense kiss of her life. As if their tongues spoke a language of their own, communicating perfectly with one another.

She closed her eyes and allowed the sensations to

take over as her hands roamed freely. So what if they were breaking the law by trespassing. Who cared if they were stranded in a blizzard. The only thing that mattered was them.

She raked her nails over the ridges of back muscles, loving the hard planes of his body. It would be too easy to lose herself in the moment, to let the chemistry and sex appeal rule her. The war waged within her whether to keep going or... was there another option?

Everything felt so good. She couldn't stop; not yet. Theo wasn't the player she pegged him to be, but that didn't make her easy. She'd never moved so quickly on the physical side with someone who wasn't her boyfriend. She wasn't another puck bunny.

The battle of whether to let things progress or stop him was lost when the zipper on her jeans lowered. His fingers dove inside her panties and he rubbed her bare mound. She moaned into his mouth.

Theo brushed Carly's slit with the side of his finger, slowly exploring her folds. She should have been embarrassed by how wet she was; by how turned on she had become from a kiss. There was no denying it. Within a few swipes, his digit was drenched with her arousal.

He slipped one finger inside her and applied a heavenly amount of pressure with his palm. They continued to kiss as he explored her wet heat. Carly moaned again as Theo inserted another finger. He fingered her slowly and then faster until the climax built. His thumb flicked her clit, and she shot off the couch. He smiled against her mouth and kissed down her throat.

His pace slowed, making Carly delirious for

more. He circled her nub while pumping his fingers in and out. He latched onto her nipple, engulfing the hard tip in his heat. She was so close, getting closer with each kiss and suck he provided to her breasts. She rocked her hips against his hand, reaching for her orgasm, but he kept it out of range.

"Theo," she said, not sounding like herself. Who was this wanton woman? Carly didn't care; she needed release. "Please, make me come."

He flicked his tongue across her sensitive nipple and kissed his way to her navel. "Your wish is my command."

Yes! She expected him to finger her until she shattered, but he removed his hand.

She whimpered in protest and lifted her hips to chase his hand. He pulled at her pants and panties, lowering them past her butt. She wiggled her hips to help him remove her clothes, leaving her exposed from the waist down. He drew off each of her socks and he added the items to an ever-growing pile on the floor.

Theo sat back on his heels and pushed her knees apart. She wanted to close them, but the way he admired her body made her feel beautiful, not embarrassed. He lifted her leg and kissed his way up from her ankle to the top of her right thigh, then repeated on the left. With both of her legs draped over his shoulders, he pressed his nose into the bare flesh and inhaled.

"Damn, that's good. I hope you're ready." Without more fanfare, he licked along her entrance. One long, torturous stroke.

A shiver raced across her spine. He used his fingers to part her folds, then he licked Carly's entire length before kissing her clit.

There was so much she wanted to do. Lock her legs and capture him there forever, open them wider to give him full access, and scream his name all at the same time. Instead, she sat up on her elbows to watch. Theo's shaggy brown hair bobbed between her legs as he tasted her. His tongue worked its magic, reaching deep inside. He added his fingers into the fray and Carly became a writhing mess within seconds. He devoured her pussy and kept going.

His fingers penetrated her while he circled her clit with his tongue. He started slow but increased his speed quickly. Carly clenched against him as her climax neared. He must have sensed it too because he doubled his efforts and sucked her clit hard.

"Oh... Theo... Oh..." She splintered into a million pieces and shot off like a firework display on New Year's Eve. She entered the land of bright lights and sparkles.

Theo slowed but didn't stop until he'd wrung every last ounce of her orgasm from her. Once her head fell back onto the couch like a useless rag doll, he put her back onto the cushion. He kissed her body, and paid homage to her breasts again, but not for long.

"That was... I can't talk yet, but give me a minute and I'm sure I can be clever."

Theo chuckled, and the sound crushed the last of Carly's defenses. He wedged his body beside her, his head propped on his arm, while the other traced an unknown pattern on her skin. He trailed his fingers down the center of her chest, across her ribs and up her arms. His gentle touch left goosebumps in its wake.

This amazing man had given her the best orgasm of all time. She'd never come so hard or for so long. She wasn't a virgin, and this wasn't her first oral experience, but this was far and away the most explosive.

Would she be able to repay the favor, did he expect that?

She needed to catch her breath before she could try. She also needed a heavy dose of courage, it had been a long while since she'd pleasured a man, and the truth was she'd only been with boys. High school boys who'd got off almost as soon as she touched them.

Theo wasn't cut from the same cloth as those guys.

She twisted to face him and followed his lead, using her fingers to trace a similar pattern on his body.

He closed his eyes, and Carly could tell he was enjoying her touch. She repeated his actions several times before her hand traveled down his abs and traced the top of his jeans. His erection strained against the zipper, needing to be released. She lowered her hand, ready to free him, but he stopped her.

"What's wrong?" She wanted to give back. Make him fall apart and unravel like he'd done to her.

"We can go slow, Carly."

"I don't get it." Her confusion was written all over her face. "Don't you want me… want me to touch, you know…" It was impossible to talk about that kind of thing with Theo Montagne.

He lifted her hand and kissed her palm. "You asked me to make you come, and I wanted to make you feel good. I couldn't resist tasting you and feeling your body contract against my face. So pretty. But I don't want to rush things. It's obvious you have some wildly incorrect notions of who I am, so let me prove myself. Let's get to know each other."

Those words were sweet and totally unnecessary. "I thought we were doing that," she said, looking down at the bulge in his pants. "Maybe I want to make you feel good too."

"Perfect, because you are." He adjusted her bra and pulled her shirt back down to cover her breasts. "I really like you Carly, and I wouldn't want you to regret anything. Trust me, I would love nothing more than to make love to you, but it's too soon. I'm not looking for a quickie, plus, I don't want you to think I'm a player."

"I don't think that anymore," she corrected him.

He hugged her, an act more intimate than the kissing. "Good. Turn over."

She turned over, and he pulled her body against his, angling their bodies so they were spooning on the couch.

Her back settled against his front. He reached onto the back of the couch and pulled a blanket over them. "You're not the first person to misjudge me. I'm always under public scrutiny," Theo said, resting his chin on the top of her head. "Every move I make is public knowledge. People can be royal pricks and they will judge us."

"Us? I'm not exactly famous. No one will care we're friends." The word friends didn't fit, but she wasn't prepared to think of them as anything more.

"They care. Why is anyone's guess? But they'll want to know everything about you. Like what you do for fun, who your friends are, and they'll dig into your past. So, is there anything you'd like to tell me before we continue this relationship?"

"We are not in a relationship," she reminded him.

"Yet," he corrected her.

She elbowed his ribs lightly. "Damn, you're smug. If you want to know who I am then ask; don't make it sound like my life's story will be headline news."

"Tell me about yourself. Consider me a fan." His playfulness penetrated her defenses.

She found herself wanting to open up, but had no idea what to say. "There's not much to tell; I'm a redneck country girl with a wicked aim, so don't mess with me." Her joke made Theo's grip stiffen. Telling a guy, she knew how to use a gun and could shoot him might not be the best way to win him over. Not that she wanted to impress Theo. "I'm kidding; a little. Most of my time is spent at university studying, and the rest at work to pay for it. I live a very common and boring life."

He relaxed. "It's not boring to me. Tell me more." Their bodies were so close that she could feel his chest expand as he breathed.

"Um… I moved to Winnipeg this past summer and I haven't made many friends yet. Okay, I have two. My roommate, Beth, and my co-worker, Miranda. Both girls are cuckoo for hockey which we have in common. They pretty much had to become my friends." Admitting she wasn't miss popular was embarrassing when she was sitting next to Theo. He oozed charm in his sleep she'd bet. Everyone loved him.

"Moving to a new city is tough. I've only lived here a few years, and I have a shit-ton of acquaintances but only a handful of friends. So, I get it."

"No way!" She was shocked and wanted to turn over, but she didn't.

He chuckled at her high-pitched outburst. "My first year, I was home sick and spent all my time off traveling back to Montreal to visit my family and my girl. This season, I have no reason to go back there. It's been pretty lonely."

The mention of his ex-girlfriend and Theo being lonely caused her to stir. "How did your ex handle the limelight?"

He laughed again, and the sound caressed her body like a sip of hot chocolate. "Not well I'm afraid."

"I can't picture you sitting at home alone. That image doesn't gel with your public persona." A vision of him alone and sprawled naked on his bed popped into her head. His hand on his cock as he... bad Carly. She swallowed and clenched her knees together.

"We have an entire team dedicated to building our public image. Say this; wear that; it's exhausting, but it's all part of the gig." He blew out a big breath.

That didn't sound fun. "I wouldn't enjoy that very much. Must be tedious." Here he was telling her how much life with him sucked and she couldn't stop thinking about sucking something else.

"Parts of it can be, but I've stayed on their good books, so they leave me alone for the most part. But new relationships are always a topic of conversation." Theo tucked a loose curl behind her ear. His finger lingered against her neck. "I like the hint of red in your hair and the freckles here."

The compliment made her blush. "You shouldn't have to debate who you are friends with. It's none of their business."

"You're wrong. Dating me isn't simple or easy."

Dating Theo Montagne. The idea sent a tingle through her body, but he wasn't the guy for her. The conversation seemed far too intense; too meaningful. "You're Mr. Complicated now. Is that it?"

"I'm a kid from Montreal who gets to play pro-hockey. The complicated part is the world that surrounds hockey. Think you can handle it?"

Carly loved a challenge, but this was one she shouldn't take. It was a game she couldn't win, but it would be so much fun to play. She remained quiet, refusing to answer.

A few minutes passed. "Goodnight, Carly. Sweet dreams."

"Goodnight, Theo." They cuddled, and she watched the snow fall. His breathing evened out, and she fell asleep wrapped in his arms.

CHAPTER NINE

The room was too warm and Carly couldn't move. Her arms were pinned. His body pressed against hers, holding her hostage in a cocoon of heat. She smiled and turned her head. Theo's face was right there, their noses practically touching.

He was striking.

Carly slowly freed one arm and swept the hair off his forehead. Careful not to wake him, and risk losing her chance to gaze at him while he slumbered next to her. The overnight hair growth on his chin suited him. He seemed at peace and the soft snore was more cute than annoying.

What a different start to the day compared to the previous one. The lonely ache in her chest was gone. The painful void remained, but it had lessened, become bearable. She didn't know what to make of that.

Theo's mouth opened slightly, and she noticed more tiny scars, besides the obvious one on his lip. They hid in his hairline and brow, and another across his chin. He wore battle wounds from his sport.

Carly wanted to pinch herself, to confirm this was real. Normal girls like her didn't sleep with guys who looked like Theo. The famous statue of David had nothing on this man. A priceless work of art, imperfections and all.

He wasn't perfect, and neither was she. Except, he wasn't an ordinary guy; he was a hockey hero to millions of adoring fans. Never mind the famous millionaire part, she couldn't believe the league's top player was the same man who'd held her all night long.

There was no time for regrets. She might never get the chance to be carefree again. Be the girl to let loose, have fun and not worry about expectations and commitments. Having the best grades, taking everything seriously and over planning had gotten her nowhere.

She removed the blanket and let it fall to the floor. The first thing she wanted him to see would be her; the first thing he felt to be her lips. She moved to her side to face him and pressed her lips to his. She woke him with a kiss.

A kiss that started off slow, but then he kissed back. She didn't even care they hadn't brushed their teeth; he tasted great. She expected to give him a peck, something sweet, but it turned into a kiss steamier than a pot of boiling water. It quickly built until she was on the verge of climax.

She felt something hard poke against her stomach. She reached to stroke him, but he stopped her hand and pressed it over his heart. The steady thud let her know he was equally turned on.

"Good morning," he said, stretching his legs.

"Let's make it an even better morning." She winked, finding her bold side.

"It's not that I wouldn't love to have your hands on me. I want that more than you know, Carly. But I want more too." He kissed the tip of her nose. "I don't want a shadow of doubt to cross your mind when you think of me, or of us together."

She wiggled closer until no space came between them. "I feel good about us. I want to live in the present, whatever happens tomorrow, we can figure it out then." She kissed his lips, ran her tongue over the seam until he opened to her. She sucked on his tongue, making him growl. Low and deep like a primal call to mate. This was a call she was more than willing to answer.

"I want you, Theo." Her attempt to free her hands failed.

"I can see the hesitation in your eyes," he said, and she blinked any doubt away. She raised her brow in challenge. He laughed. "Trust me, it's there. If it weren't, we'd find a bed immediately."

A bed - yes please.

Theo gave her a quick peck on the lips before rolling over her and getting off the couch. They each took turns in the main floor bathroom. Neither of them had ventured anywhere upstairs, and she was okay keeping it that way. She brushed her teeth with her finger and after using the toilet, she came out to find Theo standing by the window watching the snow.

Carly joined him, wrapping her arms around his midsection. "No signs of stopping." The statement floated through the air like a promise. They had more time.

They stood there for a while, holding one another and watching the winter wonderland outside unfold.

"Did you check the power?" She asked, walking over to the coffee table and picking up her phone. He shook his head. "No power yet." And no service, she confirmed with her phone.

"Guess we'll be here a while longer." His lips kicked up on one side. The devil himself crafted Theo's mouth for sin, it was that wicked.

"What should we do?" She bit her lip, trying to suggest they find that bedroom.

He didn't take the bait. "Come sit with me." He took her hand and pulled her to sit on his lap. "Merry Christmas." He gripped the back of her head and kissed her softly. There was no tongue, but it wasn't necessary.

Carly pressed her forehead against Theo's and looked into his eyes. "Merry Christmas. Tell me your best and worst Christmas stories." She wanted to learn more about him. Every detail. "Go back as far as you need to." She snuggled onto his legs and wrapped her arms around his neck.

He scratched his chin. "Hmm. You go first while I pick one."

Carly didn't have to ponder for long, she knew her favorite.

"I was ten, and my dad handed me a present wrapped with red and green stripes. He was excited about it, almost giddy, which if you knew my dad, would not fit. Anyway, I tore through that wrapping paper and inside the wooden box was the last thing I expected. I mean, it wasn't at all what I wanted. I asked for a pink Barbie Dream House set. What I ended up with was this piece of metal and a box of bullets. He bought me a gun."

Theo rubbed her leg, probably thinking this was the worst Christmas story, it wasn't.

"At first sight, I hated it, but I smiled even though I wanted to cry. My dad thought he hit it out of the park. Once he'd explained the reason, I had to agree, he nailed it. Dad said he would teach me to shoot, and then we could hunt together someday. He gave me a gun, but what he really gave me was his time. I rarely saw him during the week, because he worked so much, but he promised to take me to the range and teach me how to shoot. He took me every weekend that year, and we've hunted lots since."

She couldn't tell what Theo thought, but he was smiling, which she took as a good sign. Carly wished her dad was sitting there with them. He would love Theo. Not because he played hockey, although that gave him extra brownie points, but because he was genuine.

"That was both sweet and a tiny bit scary. It's clear you loved him and wanted to please him. For a young kid that was pretty cool of you to give up the Barbie whatever you called it in exchange for a gun. I wouldn't have taken that as well as you did."

His lips caressed the sensitive skin under her ear. "Is it wrong of me to think it's sexy that you can shoot?" His hand roamed under her shirt, trailing his fingertips against her stomach.

Carly never considered herself sexy. Cute as in girl next door, yes, but bad ass, no. "I'm glad you approve. Your turn."

Theo drew a circular pattern against her skin. "No, tell me your least favorite and then I'll go." He licked along the shell of her ear.

"I... can't think about anything but you, when you're doing that."

He nibbled on her lobe. "Good, but I'll stop, for now," he said, and she wanted to protest, tell him to keep going but she was learning fast that Theo had a stubborn side.

"Last year, was a low one for me. I'd received some devastating news and even the holidays couldn't bring me out of my funk. Your turn." She should have made up a story. Told him about the year she fell off the rocking horse her grandfather had made her. Spending the entire day in the emergency room was horrible, however, that didn't come close to last years.

"I'm sorry. Care to elaborate, I feel like there's more to the story."

Carly shrugged her shoulders. "I don't want to talk about it, Christmas is supposed to be magical, so let's focus on the happier ones. No more dodging, you're up." She rubbed her hands together, getting ready for a juicy tale.

He tilted her chin towards him and their eyes locked.

"Whenever you're ready, I've been told I'm a decent listener."

He kissed her tenderly. "I'm glad this one isn't your worst. Because... My favorite Christmas to date is this one. It's the first one I'm spending with you."

Implying first of many she hoped. No sweeter words had ever been said. The vault of her heart opened a crack. The flutter in her stomach complicated things.

They kissed, and she had to admit this Christmas

was quickly becoming a contender for the top spot.

CHAPTER TEN

The morning gave way to the afternoon as the storm continued. They had done little more than make-out like two horny kids who'd discovered the pleasures of French-kissing. She would have been happy to kiss the day away. But Theo suggested they go dig out the car and survey the area with the brightness of day on their side.

She wagered the real reason he wanted to go outside, was because he was having a hard time refusing her constant advances. Any other girl might have been put out by his refusal to take the next step but Carly found it endearing. It didn't, however, reduce her desire to see him naked and do nasty things with him. Every kiss, every touch made her crazy for more. She didn't understand how he had so much willpower.

They dressed to go outside and Carly once again loved the way his hair curled out from under his hat. He looked so young and virile, like a man ready to conquer the world. For now, he'd have to settle for battling the elements.

The blizzard was bound to stop at some point; a fact that made Carly uneasy. Only yesterday, she'd been desperate for clear skies, and now the prospect wasn't as appealing. Theo was one hundred percent behind her shift in perception.

Two steps out the front door and Carly wanted to turn back. It was cold and miserable.

Mother Nature continued her quest to cover the earth in white, but had slowed her pursuit somewhat. The wind howled and whipped flakes in her face. Visibility was still poor, but not as bad as the previous evening.

Snow drifts had formed against the side of the house, reaching the top of the windows. She guesstimated the snowfall amount as well over a foot. The only brightness Carly found was Theo's smiling face.

"What is there to smile about? There's so much snow," she grumbled as the freshly fallen powder reached her mid-calf.

"I'm here with you, and I've been dreaming of a white Christmas." He spun her around in a twirl while singing. "Just like—"

"Don't quit your day job, Casanova," Carly interrupted his serenade before it got started. Theo might be a professional hockey player, but he couldn't hold a note to save his life. She giggled at finally finding something he wasn't perfect at.

"Glad you find me entertaining." He pulled her close and kissed the top of her snow-covered head.

Hand in hand, they made their way towards the mountain of snow that hid the car. Not a speck of red could be detected. Carly shivered, thinking about what might have happened to them if they hadn't gotten off the road when they did. Their decision to turn around had been a good one. There's no way they would have made it to the city in one piece.

Carly used her arm to wipe the sticky snow from off the car door. Theo reached inside and took out a brush. The small blue stick looked incapable of dealing with the massive amount of snow, but Theo made it work. Carly used her hands to help dig, and in no time, they had dug out his car.

The red paint glared at her, reminding her their time would soon be ending. But it wasn't over yet. The fresh snow and gusting winds made their effort seem in vain. The sports car wouldn't stand a chance plowing through the drifts to get back on the main roads.

"We should go find shovels," Theo suggested as he looked at the snow-covered driveway.

They had their work cut out for them, but shoveling before the winds tapered off would be an exercise in futility. "Any progress we make now will be swept away by that wind. We'll check back a little later."

"Good point." Theo bent down and Carly admired his fine behind.

The goodbye might be harder than she envisioned, she wasn't ready yet. She looked down and stomped her boots to remove the snow buildup. The snow stuck to her mittens. It would be the right consistency for building a snowman. She was about to make that suggestion when a blur of white whizzed by her head. Snowballs were another option.

"Game on, hockey star."

Carly dashed around the car for cover. It didn't take long to create a small arsenal of balls and when she lifted her head, another ball buzzed her. Theo had good aim, but hers was better, and he'd given away his location.

Without looking, she stood up and pelted six balls in his direction. Five connected and she couldn't help but laugh at his wide blue eyes and stunned expression. One shot landed on his chin, dusting his beard in white fluff. She might look like a girly-girl but she grew up in the country, raised by parents who wanted a son. He didn't stand a chance.

Theo dropped the one snowball he was about to throw and raised his hands in defeat. "You win. I surrender."

She could hardly believe a man as competitive as a pro hockey player would accept losing so quickly. Carly stepped out from behind the car. Theo rushed her and they both went tumbling to the ground. She would have been mad if she wasn't so busy laughing. He covered her body with his, pinning her arms by her sides with his knees, and he sprinkled snow on her face.

"Stop, cheater," she yelled, blinking snow from her eyes.

His laugh grew louder as she wiggled to get free. She shook her head from side to side, but it was no use, he would only stop when he was ready. She eventually stopped struggling. "All right, you win." She wasn't only talking about their game. Theo was winning her heart.

"That's right," he said through his laughter. He lowered his upper body until their faces were inches apart. "You look like an angel right now. Sparkling and so damn pretty my eyes hurt." He didn't give her a chance to respond before kissing her and stealing her words with his mouth.

Theo made it clear he wasn't interested in a fling, but could she offer more? Was she ready? Kissing him, made her feel like anything was possible. He rolled off and flapped his arms in the snow.

"What are you doing, crazy man?"

"Making snow angels, what else?" He stood up and surveyed his handiwork. "Not bad, but it doesn't compare to your beauty."

She laughed at how ridiculous they were being, but she had to admit he made a good angel. At some point, she stopped looking at the snow and the blizzard as the end of the world, and became thankful for every flake.

Theo was changing her view of things, and that had to be a good thing. For so long she'd been acting like a drill sergeant with her life. She allotted no time for fun, because she wanted to please everyone around her, and atone for her mistakes. It seemed like she couldn't do anything right no matter how hard she tried.

Lying in the snow, her stomach twisted with guilt. She hadn't checked her phone once in the last hour. She was the world's worst, most inconsiderate child. Here she was having the time of her life, certain her parents were worrying themselves sick. Carly scrambled to her feet and tugged on Theo's arm, pulling him towards the house.

"Let's go back inside."

"Sounds good, I've worked up an appetite. You?" His smile was infectious.

"Sure."

Once inside she didn't bother taking off her coat before rushing for her phone. There was still no service. She breathed a sigh of relief, but the sadness didn't dissipate. It clung to her like an unwelcome tick.

Theo wasn't all thumbs in the kitchen as Carly would have suspected a twenty-year-old man to be. He made a decent PB&J sandwich. A little chocolate would have rounded off the meal, but there was none in the kitchen or front closets. They checked twice. He laughed at her disappointment, but told her he'd buy her a giant slab of it when they got out. She wouldn't hold him to that, but thinking about chocolate soothed her. The way Theo doted on her, made her feel like a princess.

Lunch turned out to be nothing like her usual Christmas meal with all the trimmings, but Theo made it special all the same. He lit candles even though the brightness of the day illuminated the room fine. This time he sat next to her and held her hand under the table. The gesture sent the butterflies dancing in her stomach again.

"Did you always love hockey?" She asked before taking her first bite.

"Since the moment I put on skates, I've been chasing a puck. I remember the first game I saw on TV, I was two maybe three, and I've been in love ever since."

"Why?" Carly liked hockey because her dad did. It was a way for them to bond and somewhere along the way she became a fan.

"I've never really thought about why. Most Canadian kids grow up playing hockey and wanting to play for the NHL. My dad had all of us boys in skates as soon as we learned to walk. As a kid, I used to watch hours of hockey reels, learning how the pros skated, passed, checked, everything. I wasn't satisfied until I could replicate their moves. I love everything about the sport."

"So, you're one of the few who got to see his childhood dream come true. I thought most players go pro for the accolades, and of course the fat paycheck," she said with a giggle. She finished her sandwich and watched as Theo ate his third.

"I love how the fans cheer, don't get me wrong that's a bonus. The money is all right too. But, I couldn't imagine doing anything else. The scary part once you make it, is how quickly it can all fall apart. I'm one injury away from losing my dream. I'm one bad season away from it all ending. It's terrifying."

Carly squeezed Theo's hand. "You're an amazing player. I don't think you have to worry about not getting another contract. You've got a long career ahead of you."

"I hope so, but you never know. I thought getting drafted in the first round was cool but my mom wasn't there to share that moment. My dad and manager kind of ruined the fun with the money talk. I mean, I care about making money, but I care more about playing."

"Your dad was most likely looking out for you, making sure you weren't getting taken advantage of. I hear things in pro sports can get pretty cutthroat."

"You have no idea how much pressure rests on these shoulders."

Theo would be surprised how much she could relate to the pressure of being the best and pleasing everyone. They had so much more in common than she would have ever imagined.

"Well let me relieve some of your stress by cleaning up. You can go relax."

Theo smiled. "I won't argue with that. Thanks Carly, you're the best." He rounded the table and kissed her cheek. He disappeared, leaving her with a few plates and a lot of information to digest.

She ran the water and a soapy cloth over the butter knife and it all felt so domestic, like playing house. Carly pictured living with Theo and sharing similar lunches on lazy days. Kicking back after a heavy school day, snuggled on a couch and watching a game together. She laughed out loud at her daydream.

Theo told her earlier, he hadn't had a good Christmas since his mom passed away, and she planned to change that. She tried to think of something she could do to make this one good for him. The more he divulged about himself, the more she knew he was a genuine good guy. He deserved to have the best Christmas.

She pondered her options, getting lost in the possibilities. All paths ended with them in a bed. If she gave herself to him, would she be able to walk away after?

She liked Theo, more than she'd set out to. If she was being honest, she could so easily fall for him. He had so many great qualities to love. However, there was a big part of her that didn't trust him. She didn't trust herself. She'd been down a similar road before, with disastrous results.

Her musing got interrupted by Theo dropping a kiss against the back of her neck. Shivers of anticipation raced down her spine. "Come with me," he said, taking her hand and leading her out of the room.

The energy shifted between them, became more sexually charged, and her entire body was primed for him. The eagerness for them to move their relationship forward monopolized her thoughts, leaving her senses on high alert.

Her mind was made up. She knew what to do in order to make this his best Christmas, and she hoped he would go along with her plans.

CHAPTER ELEVEN

C arly listened to the loud pounding of her heart and wondered if Theo heard it. His giant hand engulfed hers, making her feel petite. This was it. They were going to have sex. Theo walked her into the living room and pointed towards the couch.

A pang of disappointment settled in her gut when he didn't sit with her, or take her to a bedroom, as she had stupidly hoped for.

All was not lost. She could take the reins and explain herself. Her attraction to him was more than skin deep and she was ready to move beyond the kissing. Last night he'd rocked her world with his fingers and tongue, but she craved more. He thought she wasn't ready, but he was wrong. Carly had never been more certain about anything.

"Theo, please come sit with me." She held out her hand, but he didn't take it.

The confident, at times arrogant, man was sweating. A sheen of perspiration collected at his hairline. He wiped his hands on his jeans and breathed heavily. If Carly didn't know better, she would think he was nervous.

But what would he have to be apprehensive about? Her mind jumped to the only logical conclusion.

A cold sweat beaded on her brow. During their time together, Carly had learned how caring and thoughtful Theo could be. The only thing that explained his behavior was regret. He regretted messing around with her and now, he dreaded telling her. The kissing, the fooling around, all the shenanigans would end now.

Carly closed her eyes, and took a deep breath. Theo had done the impossible, and made her like a hockey player. She considered him a friend with the potential for more. Her hand dropped to her lap, and she knotted her fingers together.

Sex with no strings attached was the perfect way to prove to herself that she wasn't as damaged as she thought. Or it could confirm her worst fears. Looking into the deep blue sea of his eyes, she knew he was worth the risk.

Her eyes darted past him as he shuffled from foot to foot searching for his words. The snow hadn't stopped yet. From her seat on the couch, the visibility appeared too poor to drive. Elation rose from the pit of despair at the joy of each frozen crystal. Christmas wasn't over yet, and she might still have her chance to get closer to him. Intimately closer at least because she had nothing else to offer.

He cleared his throat. "Okay, so... Um, I have a present for you."

What? How could he have brought her a

present?

"Don't get too excited, it's nothing fancy, it's not even something you can open. None the less, I hope you like it since it wouldn't feel like an official Christmas without presents. Here is a gift from my heart to yours."

He smiled, and she returned the sentiment. She kept her hands folded on her lap, waiting for him to give her a gift. Something from his heart.

"Here goes nothing. I wanted to quote one of my favorite poems by Lord Byron, entitled She Walks in Beauty, but I only remembered the first few lines."

He lowered himself onto bent knees and took her shaking hands in his. Theo kissed her knuckles, and Carly sensed the romance sprinkled through the air like a magical mist. His eyes locked onto hers and there was no place on Earth she would have rather been in that moment than with Theo.

"When I look at you, I see the purity of your soul, the exquisite radiance of your smile, and the glow that surrounds you. You are the perfect woman he describes. Carly, you walk in beauty, and everything else pales by comparison. Not because of your gorgeous exterior, but because of the tenderness, the darkness and light that shines from within you."

He spoke like a poet and natural storyteller. Carly was mesmerized by his words as much as the blue of his eyes. She could sit there and listen to the soft purr of his voice for hours. He paused and chewed his lower lip. She remained silent, waiting with bated breath for what he would say next.

"I wish I remembered the lines for you, but you inspired me to find my own words. Byron must have had his own version of Carly Saint when he wrote that piece."

"Theo," she whispered. It was her turn to clear her throat. His words affected her deeply. "Your words are beautiful. Thank you for my present."

"Oh, there's more. We learned Byron back in high school and that opening stanza always struck a chord, but I didn't fully understand it, until I met you. Anyway, the next poem is mine, inspired by you. Please remember I'm a hockey player not a poet."

She wasn't sure she could listen to anymore without passing out. All the blood had already rushed to her lower half, leaving her woozy. No matter what he came up with, she already loved every word he'd said.

"The stars aligned, bringing us together, some will call it fate,

I agree, because I'm falling for you, without having had a first date.

You are the entire package wrapped in a sassy little bow,

I will cherish our time forever and always remember the snow.

A poet, I'm not, but what can I say,

Except, I'm glad we are together, and Happy Holiday."

He brought her hands to his lips and kissed her knuckles. His eyes searching hers for a reaction.

Theo Montagne wrote her a poem. The best present of all time.

"Wow, Theo. Thank you." She placed their joined hands over her heart. Carly was blown away by his sensitive side. The way he described her and said she reminded him of one of the most romantic poems ever written was both hauntingly beautiful and heartfelt. "That was lovely. Your words will forever be etched into my heart."

Theo's cheeks turned rosy at the compliment. "It was far from spectacular, but I'm glad you liked it."

Carly more than liked it. It was over the top swoon-worthy. "I did." No one had ever done anything like that for her before. She doubted she would ever meet someone who would again.

He held her hands and looked right into her eyes. The piercing blue digging deep into her soul. "Can I ask you something, Carly?"

"Anything," she said breathlessly.

"Do you find it strange how comfortable we are around one another?"

She swallowed the lump in her throat. The conversation, the present, all of it wasn't about sharing something minor or insignificant. Theo was making a play for her heart. The one thing she did not want to give up. Her body, she was ready and willing to give. She was aching for them to connect physically, but this was too emotional for her.

He waited for a response, but she wasn't able to answer.

"I know you feel it too. It's like I can be myself without fear of judgment. The hockey world expects me to be a certain way. My family has similar expectations. I'm still learning how to deal with it, you know."

Carly knew exactly what he was talking about. All her life, she'd felt like she had to behave a certain way, and somewhere she lost herself within those expectations. Her outward appearance didn't match the geek inside.

"I get it, growing up isn't easy. Navigating the

waters into adulthood has been tougher than I expected too."

"Yeah…" A wistful look crossed his face. This hockey player had a heart, and he was burrowing his way inside hers.

She cupped his face in her hands. "Thank you again for my present. It moved me, more than I can express through words." Her lips met his in a kiss she hoped conveyed how affected she was.

"Merry Christmas, Carly."

"It's time for your present now," she said, rising to her feet. She found her courage. If he pushed past his fear and recited poetry, she could give herself to him. Carly figured it was time to put her big girl panties on and tell Theo what she wanted. Show him what she wanted from him.

He was still kneeling in front of her as she lifted her shirt over her head. Her eyes remained locked on his. His sharp intake of breath confirmed he hadn't been expecting this. Before she changed her mind, she unclasped her bra and let it fall to the floor by Theo's legs.

"You said, you wanted to wait, but we've waited long enough. I have no fancy words or sentimental gestures to offer. But I am offering myself." It sounded so much more pathetic than it had in her mind.

"Breathtaking. I am in awe of you." He kissed her stomach, right above her jeans. His hands roamed over her ass, squeezing her round globes. "Are you one hundred percent sure?"

She nodded.

"Then take off your pants and panties and let me see you. All of you." The command sent a jolt of desire right to her core.

She got the distinct impression he meant more than her naked body; he wanted everything. After this moment, there would be no going back. Bared and vulnerable, and she wouldn't have wanted things any other way.

Theo sat back on his legs and watched her. His eyes roamed over her curves, making her feel every bit as beautiful as his earlier words. She reached for the fly on her jeans and undid the button and zipper. A hint of her red panties peeked through the opening. He leaned in and kissed the top of her mound. This emboldened her further to continue showing him all of her.

Carly hooked her fingers into the waistband of her jeans and panties and lowered them to the ground, exposing her most private parts. He helped her remove the articles along with her socks. She stood before him completely naked.

Her first reaction was to cover herself. To hide, but she forced her arms to remain by her side as she presented herself to him. Theo devoured her with hungry eyes. There was no mistaking the attraction within those blue orbs. The attention made her hot, and she knew he could see the arousal glistening down below. With every passing second her desire grew thicker. The anticipation of his touch was killing her.

"The most exquisite present I have ever received. Carly, your body deserves to be cherished and I plan to do that. Will you let me make love to you?"

Why did he have to call it love? The joining of their bodies would be fun and hot as hell but it wasn't love. She didn't know how to make him understand.

She'd have to convey her message through words and body language. Love didn't factor into the equation.

"Touch me, Theo. I want to feel you inside me, I want to look into your eyes when I make you come. I want this to be a Christmas, neither of us will ever forget."

He didn't move, Theo said nothing as he stared at her. Each second that passed, her pulsed raced faster until it was all she heard. Carly wondered if she'd made a mistake. Had she read the signs all wrong? Would giving him her body be enough or was he set on her giving more?

The scrutiny of his gaze heated her from the inside out. The silence swallowed her last shred of courage. She looked at him, waiting for him to decide whether she was enough.

CHAPTER TWELVE

Theo's quiet assessment skyrocketed her arousal, the moisture practically dripped down her leg. From his position, he saw everything. Carly had never been so wet in her entire life, and he hadn't touched her. Yet. The anticipation drove her crazy.

As the seconds stretched on, she nervously shuffled from one from foot to the next. Theo's eyes never left her body, combing over every inch. It seemed like an eternity before he finally broke the silence and rose from his knees.

"Carly, my sweet, undeniably sexy girl, you have bewitched me." He closed the distance between them and kissed her hard.

Their tongues intertwined as his hands touched her everywhere. Her neck, her back, her sides, she was on sensation overload. Carly tore at the hem of his sweater, lifting it. Theo removed the barrier and their bodies rejoiced in the skin to skin contact.

Her nipples were hard from the cool air of the

room, but tightened even more so as they raked against his ribs. He was so tall and powerful, she felt breakable, but she trusted him not to hurt her. Her hands roamed the broad expanse of his back while he went straight for her ass. He cupped her globes hard and thrust his erection against her stomach. Theo wanted this to happen as badly as she did.

He broke away from her mouth and they were both panting. "I want to take this slow, savor you and worship you, but I'm afraid I won't be able to. Our first time together should be special, not a quickie on the couch."

It didn't matter to Carly where they had sex as long as it happened soon. Their fingers threaded together, and he kissed her knuckles. Leading her by the hand, he pulled her away from the couch. He asked her to stand by the Christmas tree as he lit the candles on the table and threw a blanket and some pillows on the floor by her feet.

"If you're my present, it's only right I open you under the tree." The cheeky glint in his eyes and the smirk on his face reminded her of that first moment their eyes connected in the parking lot. She'd pegged him as an arrogant prick, but she'd been wrong. "Sit down for me, Carly."

Without words, she sat on the makeshift bed and looked up at him. Theo stood a few feet away and removed the rest of his clothing. It was now her turn to gawk. His abs were ripped, the deep v leading to an impressive cock. Long and thick, and all hers for the taking. Carly licked her lips, wondering what Theo would do next.

He fisted his cock, and she envied his hand. He smirked and slid it along his shaft, rounding over the tip. "You like what you see, Carly?"

She did. Very much. "Yes," she admitted.

His smile deepened at her admission. He was so sexy. "Spread your legs."

She planted her feet on the blanket, opened her legs and let her knees fall to the side. She was surprised how unabashed she was, considering it had been over a year since she'd last had sex. On the outside, she looked like every other woman, but inside she was a mess. But he wouldn't be able to see that.

His eyes flared and fixed onto her wet pussy lips. The reaction he gave was all she needed to turn things up a notch. She toyed with her taught nipple with one hand, and let the other run between her breasts, over her stomach and through the slick folds.

Theo inhaled sharply, and his pupils dilated. He liked what she was doing. She watched his hand increase in speed as she pushed one finger inside herself. The wet slurping noise should have embarrassed her but didn't. Theo stalked towards her and stopped when her face was only inches from his erection.

"Wrap those pretty lips around my cock and keep touching yourself as you suck me off." The sweet poetry reciting Theo had given way to a dirty boy, and Carly liked it. She liked it a lot.

She pinched her nipple one last time, more for a confirmation of reality than for pleasure, but it provided both. He guided his cock to her mouth and ran it over her lips, wetting them with his pre-cum. She inhaled his musky masculine aroma, and she wanted more of it. Her tongue darted out and licked the last of the moisture. Theo groaned.

He tasted mighty fine. Carly opened her mouth and Theo fed himself to her. Slowly, one inch at a time, until he hit the back of her throat. She gagged but recovered quickly. Relaxing her throat, she took a little more.

"Damn, that's good." Theo's encouragement spurred her into action and she worked her pussy faster.

She would not last long. She squeezed his ass as her tongue worked along his shaft. He pulled out and pushed back in again, each time going deeper than the last. Theo set the pace, and she let him fuck her mouth as slowly as he wanted because this was for him. She wanted this to be the best blowjob in the history of giving head.

The faster he moved his hips the more her pleasure increased. Carly moaned around him, making him hiss. The harder she sucked, the faster he thrust, and the wetter she got. Theo tightened his grip in her hair and fucked her face with a ruthless pace.

She liked how wild she made him. Her eyes stayed on his as he neared his climax. His butt cheeks clenched under her hand.

He tapped her shoulder, and his blue eyes implored her to stop. "Carly, I'm going to come," he said through clenched teeth.

She ignored his plea and sucked harder. Carly wanted him to let go, she was ready to taste him.

"Shit, if you don't stop I'll come in your mouth." He pumped faster, on the verge of release.

She rubbed her clit furiously with one hand, moments away from diving off the cliff herself. She moved her other hand between his legs and rubbed the sensitive flesh between his sack and anus. The added pressure was enough to send him over the edge.

His eyes closed and his head fell back as he thrust one last time, filling her mouth with his hot seed. He stopped moving, but his body shivered as he came. Knowing she could make him lose control like that, stimulated her own release. She swallowed every drop.

When he pulled away, he'd barely softened. "That was amazing. Give me your hand." He leaned down and sucked her fingers into his mouth, cleaning her wetness from them.

"Hmm. Now, lie back and let me taste you properly. I've been dying to get between those legs all day."

"Yes, please," she said and licked her swollen lips. Carly lay on the blanket and opened her legs wide for him. If Theo wanted to go down on her, she would not stop him. She was no longer afraid to admit she wanted him.

"Thank you for my present," were the last words he said before he sucked her clit into his mouth.

Her hips raised to meet him and her hands dove into his silky hair. He didn't go slow, and he didn't stop until she cried out his name. The second she contracted, he inserted two fingers and her walls clenched around him. He worked a second orgasm from her in a matter of minutes.

She was left overly sensitive and more than ready to have him fill her. "Theo, I want your cock inside me."

He smiled with her juices coating his lips as he crawled over her and kissed her. Their bodies lined up as their kiss heated. A most delicious combination of them lingered on her tongue. Her new favorite flavor. Their tongues found a slow sensual rhythm unique to them. His rock-hard cock pressed against her entrance but did not push in.

The tease against her sensitive folds wasn't enough. She craved the fullness of being taken by a man. "Theo, stop teasing me and fuck me."

"I'm not going to fuck you, Carly. I want to make love to you so bad, but we can wait if you're not ready."

She was ready in every way. Even the way he called it making love no longer mattered. The only thing that mattered was them, coming together in the most carnal way possible.

"Then, make love to me." Carly didn't need to say another word.

Theo moved off her and reached over into his jeans. She lay back under the tree as Theo ripped open a foil packet and wrapped himself in latex. She'd never felt the magic of the season so intimately before.

Theo's eyes found hers as he positioned himself over her. He used his hand to guide his cock to her entrance and coated the head with her arousal. The moment couldn't have been more perfect and Carly smiled as he filled her. She was nervous as her walls stretched to accommodate the delightful invasion.

"Everything okay, Theo?" She asked, worried something was wrong when he'd stopped.

"You feel so good, so tight and perfect," he said before his mouth covered hers.

All her apprehension melted away. Her scars weren't something he could feel, and in that moment, the past no longer haunted her. Carly knew there was no such thing as perfect, but this moment was as close as she would ever come.

Her eyes got lost in his sea of blue and she never wanted to be found. Theo entered her slowly, the stretch was uncomfortable, but not painful. When he pushed all the way inside, she was full to the point of bursting, but then he pulled out and she missed the fullness.

Their bodies learned to move as one. Soon, all she could hear was the wet noises of skin slapping skin. Everything felt incredible, like her nerve endings were getting the royal treatment. The harder he pounded his hips against hers the deeper he reached until her G-spot was being bombarded like the coast of Normandy on D-day. Her body was charged, primed and ready to explode.

He had her arms over her head, holding her there as he stared into her eyes. She couldn't look away, she didn't want to. His forehead pressed against hers, sweat dripping down his face and onto her cheek. "Keep your eyes on mine as you come. Focus on me as if nothing else matters except us."

His words pushed them both over the edge. A few deeper thrusts and she was done.

"Theo… I'm coming! Oh… Theo!" She kept her eyes open, but the rest of the world faded away. It was only them and nirvana.

"Carly…" Her name ghosted from his mouth as he emptied himself inside the condom. His twitches and pulses matched her quivers. She'd never experienced sex or anything else like that. He collapsed on top of her, and she welcomed the weight.

Their lips connected, and she knew she wouldn't

walk away from Theo as the same girl he'd met. He'd changed her, opened her heart and no matter what the future held for them, she would forever be grateful for this Christmas.

CHAPTER THIRTEEN

They lay on their bed of pillows and blankets. Their bodies partially under the Christmas tree, basking in the afterglow.

Carly contemplated whether to address the love statement or leave it. She never was a person to leave loose ends. In the heat of the moment, telling him to make love to her sounded right, but she feared she was unlovable.

She hadn't meant to trick him. A lump of insecurity formed in her stomach. She rolled away from him. Her past taught her people took what they wanted and left after. Her gut told her Theo was different, but her brain wasn't listening.

"Where does this leave us?" Carly picked up her t-shirt from the floor to cover her exposed breasts.

Theo reached over and took the top of her hands. "Don't cover yourself. I like looking at you."

Carly blushed at the compliment, but covered her chest with her arms never the less. "I'm glad you like what you see, but you didn't answer my question." She didn't want to feel discarded, but deep down she expected him to say wham bam thank you ma'am.

Theo rolled onto his side, propped his head on his arm and regarded her. His muscles were on full display and he made no motion to cover up. This guy was comfortable in his skin, and he had every right to be.

"Carly, what are you hoping to hear? I wasn't expecting any of this to happen, but I'm not upset it did, if that's what you're asking?"

She had nothing to lose except her pride, but standing naked before a hockey star already made her vulnerable. "I'm curious what this all means. Do we go back to you forgetting I exist, or is this something you want to do again?"

He smiled, chipping away at the ice she'd created around her heart a little more. "I would like to do that again very soon, and by the looks of this storm we'll have plenty of opportunities to do it again." He grabbed her hand and pulled her on top of him. His lips brushed against hers softly. "And again," he said, before his tongue licked along the seam, seeking approval to enter. Things took a heated turn from there.

Carly wasn't sure what all this meant, but she wanted the fullness of him inside her again. The feeling of being connected to someone. He hadn't mentioned after the storm, and that was most likely for the best. They could act like tomorrow didn't exist.

His kisses worked her into a frenzy. They kissed for a while longer, their bodies settling against one another on the ground. A comfortable post coital embrace. Carly wondered when the bubble would burst. She felt happy and those moments rarely lasted too long.

Theo trailed his hand down her arm. "Are you ever going to tell me why you hate jocks so much?"

It was true, she thought most jocks were selfish tools. She used to think it was all athletes, she downgraded to most because of Theo. She believed he might be the anomaly.

"I don't hate jocks per se," she answered, avoiding eye contact.

"Still don't trust me, huh?" He poked her in the ribs, finding her most ticklish spot by accident. She squirmed away, unable to stop the huge smile and giggles.

"Why would you say that?" She laughed as he continued to poke and prod her body with his long index finger.

His expression turned serious, sounding alarm bells in her head. Theo pulled her close, resting his chin on top of her head. "Something happened to you, and when you're ready, I would like to hear it. I won't press, that's not my style, but I need to know what I'm up against."

Carly never intended to tell anyone about her past. Only one other person knew her secrets. As far as she was concerned, it was her cross to bear.

The funny part was that she trusted Theo. But the thought of opening old wounds scared her. Her body stiffened, and she broke out in a cold sweat. The pain of those days would never be forgotten.

"I'm sorry, Carly. If you don't want to talk about your past, we don't have to, but I would love to get to know you. As I mentioned earlier, I've only had one girlfriend so I'm not well versed in what's appropriate and what's not in regards to dating. I want to know everything about you and I'm willing to share everything with you."

"You shared a big part of yourself with me a few minutes ago," she joked.

"Funny. I'm interested in more than your body, in case you haven't figured that part out." He squeezed her tight, the hug was both reassuring and telling. "I'm at a disadvantage on the information front; most of my life is available online. Search Theo Montagne and my history since birth is there in black and white. The private stuff, like the fact I lost my virginity at fifteen, that kind of information isn't on there, but those details are yours. Nothing is off limits."

His words scared the crap out of her. She wasn't ready for the tough conversations. "For starters, I felt your interest inside my body, and I am more than willing to feel it again, whenever you're up for it," she said while pinching his nipple.

He poked her rib again, and she giggled. "Minx." He placed his hand over hers. "I'm serious, I want no secrets between us. If we're going to make it as a couple then we should be comfortable to talk about anything."

Couple. Theo Montagne wanted to be part of a couple with her. The idea didn't suck. It was the opposite in fact.

"Fine. You want to know about my past, here goes."

Carly sat up and moved over to the couch to face Theo. She pulled the blanket over her chest, as much for warmth, as for support. Part of her didn't want to see his face and the judgment that would surely follow, but she had to gage his reaction. She needed to know if he would change his mind. She wouldn't blame him if he did.

As if sensing her desire to pull away, Theo got up and joined her on the couch. He shifted her legs onto his lap and rubbed her legs over the blanket. "Take your time, I'm listening."

"My dating history isn't much more than yours. At sixteen I thought I'd fallen in love. Our parents were friends, and my dad loved him. My boyfriend was a hockey player although not nearly as talented as you."

"Few people are," he said, earning him a glare loaded with contempt. He smiled like she was shooting rays of sunshine in his direction. "What? It's true." He had a point, but he didn't have to sound so conceited.

She rolled her eyes and continued. "We were young, and slaves to our hormones. We dated for a year before we had sex and we were together for another six months after that. He was always kind of selfish and cocky, but when you're sixteen and in lust nothing matters. I had dreams of walking down the aisle with him until the summer came and he went away to hockey camp."

Carly took a deep breath and squared her shoulders. "We broke up two weeks after he left. I showed up for a surprise visit and caught him cheating on me. He admitted it wasn't just that one time, but the entire time we were together. He bragged about all the other girls and told me I didn't measure up. Told me he never loved me and had been using me. He was a dipshit, but I was devastated. When he got back from camp, he had the nerve to show up at my house to get me back."

"You didn't though, right?"

Oh, how she wished she hadn't. "My dad let him in and told me to sit down and hear Kevin out. My dad, the guy supposed to be on my side and always have my back. Well, I wanted to make him happy, so I listened and we ended up back together."

There was the judgment she expected. A look that said: smart girl, stupid decision. "That's harsh. Guys can be fucking insensitive sometimes. I'm sorry he tainted your view of hockey players forever. We aren't all dipshits as you put it." He chuckled, and so did she.

"I wish it was only him. Kevin and I lasted a month before he got bored with me and moved on. I only took him back to make my dad happy, but every time Kevin kissed me, I would cringe, picturing him with someone else. Eventually, I healed and moved on. My next boyfriend was another stellar decision on my part. Dad liked Gabe from the start. He hunted, fished and played hockey."

"I'm sensing you have a type Miss Saint." Theo joked, but he was right. Carly had a specific type and Theo hit all her buttons.

"Guess that's a good thing for you." She leaned in and pressed a chaste kiss to his lips before sitting back to finish her tale. "Too bad for me; Gabe turned out to be a selfish douche, worse than Kevin by a mile."

"Why did you two break up? Because you moved here?"

She looked at the soft blue around his corneas, pulling strength from him. "We got pregnant a few months into the relationship. I told no one but him. He wanted me to abort, but that didn't feel right. My parents had tried for years to have more kids and couldn't. They miscarried three times. Ending things on purpose wasn't an option for me. When I told him that, he called me a slut and said the baby wasn't his. He spread some nasty rumors about me around town."

"Son-of-a-bitch." Theo sounded angry on her behalf and that was touching.

"Pretty much. He broke it off with me and slept with like five other girls in the two weeks before he finally accepted the truth. I took him back, not because I'm a glutton for punishment, but because he was the father of my unborn child. What else could I do? I was seventeen, pregnant and about to become a total disappointment to everyone. We decided not to tell anyone until we absolutely had to. I went through some dark days and Gabe got really busy with hockey. When he came around, he was mean and forceful. I was so scared to be alone that I clung to any shred of attention he gave me." Carly's hands shook over her stomach. A reflex from long ago.

"The sex was rough, like Gabe was punishing me. We lost the baby around eleven weeks when my uterus ruptured. The blood started right after sex and the doctors couldn't do anything. The relationship ended the same day while we were at the hospital getting the news. Gabe was happy, and I didn't know what I was. From that point on my opinion of jocks has been low."

"Yeah, I can see why you hold us in low regard. I'm sorry you went through that. Are you okay?" He never stopped rubbing her legs throughout her story.

Whatever she expected to see wasn't there. His eyes were full of caring and concern.

Her emotions were all over the map. She never imagined talking about all of it would be so painful. Her eyes burned as she twisted her fingers over her lap. "I moved passed it all and try not to think about any of it. The doctors said there was scarring and potential lasting side effects. They said I will have a hard time conceiving. I'll end up like my mom, unable to carry to term. It was a lot to process and I'm not sure I have. This is the first time I've ever talked about any of it." Her stiff upper lip couldn't stop the tears from falling down her cheeks.

Theo opened his arms to Carly, and she went willingly into them. He didn't have to provide her comfort, or be so understanding, but this wasn't an act. Theo had a heart the size of North America and Carly was being enveloped by it. Even though she didn't deserve him, she wanted him.

"Do you want kids someday?" She asked.

"No time soon, but one day. Why?" He held her close, her head pressed against his chest. The rhythmic sound of his heartbeat soothed the ache in hers.

"You said you wanted to see where this could go. You and me. Couples lay their cards on the table and I might not have babies. I'm damaged, Theo, and you deserve a woman who can give you everything."

He lifted her chin to face him. Their eyes locked and his widened. "You are not damaged. Never think that of yourself. You are smart, feisty and I love your honesty. You went through hell with your exes, but you came out a stronger woman. Who knows where the future will lead, but I am certain I want to see you in mine."

He said the most beautiful words. His mother would be proud.

For the first time in a long time, Carly had hope.

"I'd like you in mine too." She kissed him and that hope bloomed inside her heart.

CHAPTER FOURTEEN

Carly was getting used to the way Theo kissed, making love to her mouth. The precision thrust of his tongue against hers. She kissed him back with as much vigor and strength as she could muster. Her hands were always on him, exploring and tracing the contour of his muscles. The result was her wet and wanting more, and him hard and raring to go.

Once wasn't enough. She doubted she could ever get enough of Theo, but she didn't want to think too far ahead. Focused on the here and now, she looked to him to provide what she needed. "Do you have another condom?" She asked as she stroked the ridges of his chest.

He smiled and reached into his wallet. "Are you ready for me to make love to you again?"

His words no longer scared her. Every time he said love, the heaviness in her chest became lighter.

"Yes," she said, twirling her ponytail around her hand.

Theo's eyes romanced her body, telling a tale of naughty, delightful treats ahead. "Last one. We better make it count."

And they did.

Theo was insatiable and so full of virility. He was on a mission to prove what love felt like. They started out with her bent over the arm of the couch. He slammed into her in one fluid motion. The position opened her G-spot for him and he rammed into her hard. He chased her orgasm with powerful thrusts that moved the couch. The squeak and scratch against the hardwoods barely registered over her loud moaning.

Carly had never done more than the missionary position and she knew now she'd been missing out. The instant his fingers found her clit she came. Her internal walls squeezed and contracted around Theo. She cried out in pleasure, her face buried in a cushion muffling his name.

Theo wasn't done with her, not even close.

He pulled out of her, but only long enough to sit on the couch and pull her onto his lap. She mounted him and the new position allowed her to savor every ridge and contour of his cock as he entered her. She liked being face to face and in control of the pace.

Their lips met, and their tongues dueled as she rode him hard. With her knees on either side of him and her arms wrapped around his neck, they connected in a new way. Her climax came sooner than she thought possible. She closed her eyes and let the tornado of bliss toss her off balance, ripping through her and wreaking havoc on her heart.

"You have the best come-face, ever," he said, watching her regain her footing.

She opened her eyes, to see him smiling, his breathtaking grin was for her. "Yours is better."

Carly swiveled her hips and Theo growled. He flipped her onto her back, causing her to giggle. "Let's find out."

They went at each other like wild animals. He took her over and over until her legs went limp and they both collapsed onto the floor. Theo made her come so many times she lost count before he filled the condom with his release.

She was on the pill and even with her decreased chances of conceiving she knew it was better to be cautious. Another unplanned pregnancy would be too much for her wounded heart to handle. She wasn't sure she could survive the anguish of another loss.

After he disposed of the condom, he pulled her back into his arms. The solid muscle and strength made her feel safe. She'd become used to depending on herself and not seeking comfort. The luxury of being spooned and comforted was too much, and yet not enough.

The daylight had disappeared, giving way to night. They had spent the entire day fooling around, and Carly had never smiled so much. Her cheeks ached, along with another part of her. "Did you have a good Christmas, Theo?"

"Best ever. I loved my present, I hope you know I plan to keep it," he said, running his fingertips down her arm.

"What will you do with me?" Carly joked, wiggling her ass against his groin.

He gripped her hips and thrust behind her once.

His erection skimmed between her cheeks. "Oh, I'm sure we'll come up with something. But we ran out of rubbers." He bit her earlobe playfully and moved one hand up to cup her breast. He toyed with her nipple, elongating it.

"Theo!" She swatted his hand, but loved the sensations. "We shouldn't have sex without protection." Carly rolled onto her back and sat upright. Theo was laying on his side, staring at her like she was daft.

"There are other things we can do. Or have you already forgotten how talented I am with my tongue?" He waggled his brows and stuck out his very talented tongue at her.

Carly laughed, rising to her feet and making a run for it. She swiped a handful of clothes off the ground and headed down the hall. "You must catch me first," she yelled over her shoulder.

"You can't run, Carly. I'll find you." He was hot on her heels.

Her heart raced as she quickened her step, running until she reached the end of the hall. There was a door to a bedroom, she assumed. The other option was a dead-end. With nowhere to go, she planted her hand around the knob ready to hide inside, but not before looking back to see him.

Theo stalked towards her, slowly closing the distance. His naked body on full display and she loved it. "You know it's a bad idea to run from me, right? You'll have to be punished." He was joking around, but it made her hot all the same.

Carly made a split-second decision not to be caught yet. She gripped the handle and opened the door. "Can't punish me; if you can't catch me."

Two steps into the room, Theo wrapped his arms around her waist and lifted her into the air. They both laughed.

The clothes in her arms fell to the floor as Theo spun her around, bringing her front to his. She reached up on the tip of her toes and kissed him. Her tongue slipped into his mouth and licked along his teeth. She'd become addicted to his taste. When they broke apart, they were both panting.

"I'm falling in love with you," Theo said.

Carly wanted to believe him, but it was too fast. Insta-love didn't happen in real life. She even had a hard time being convinced when she read it in one of her beloved romance books.

"Theo…" She wasn't ready to hear him say those three little words, and she was even farther from saying them herself. It had only been a few hours since she accepted this wasn't a onetime thing. They were more than a hook up of convenience.

He pressed a finger to her lips. "It's okay. I didn't say it to make you uncomfortable or to hear it back. So, don't freak out. I'm not professing my undying love for you yet, but I get the feeling it won't take long for me to get there. It's fast and unexpected and I like that when I'm around you it's like I'm invincible. Carly, I'm happier than I've been in months." Theo smiled, and she wanted to smile back, but something caught her eye in the corner of the room.

The room was dark, but it was impossible to miss the giant life-sized poster of him plastered next to the window. An entire wall was dedicated to hockey. There were jersey's, cards, posters and different memorabilia. Several pictures were of Theo and his hockey team. She scanned the images and gasped. The slight variations of his arrogant smile and the sexy glint in his eyes she'd thought was all hers stared back. They didn't belong to her; he didn't either. She'd somehow forgotten he was a hockey heartthrob to millions of fans.

"You're very photogenic," she said, walking up to one picture where he was topless and his body had been covered in oil. He was every teenage girl's fantasy man.

Theo stepped next to her, wrapping his arm over her shoulder. "It's part of the job."

Carly stiffened. "Do you like being adored like this?" If she wanted to date him then she'd have to get used to this. There was no if; she wanted him, but this was all too much. Sharing Theo with the world and never having him all to herself.

How could she accept never being the priority?

He exhaled loudly and turned her in his arms so they were facing one another. "Not really, but it doesn't suck either. I love playing hockey. I work my ass off to be the best and with that comes this stuff." He waved his hand around, pointing at the posters and a calendar of him posed with nothing but a blanket covering his private parts. Theo didn't have a bad side, and every smoking-hot inch was displayed for the world. "Fading into the background doesn't sell tickets to the game. You don't understand the amount of work that goes into PR. We're forever chasing the cup. Carly, you—"

"You have lots of fans and you like to keep them happy. I get it. Posing half-naked somehow translates into ticket sales." She didn't like seeing these pictures and looked down at their bare feet. The bubble of lust busted wide open and out popped the reminder of NHL demands. Theo wasn't a free man. He didn't call the shots in his own life.

"I'll have you know every single one of those pictures was taken for charity." He tilted her chin, so she was forced to look into the ocean of his eyes which helped to calm her racing heart. "All the proceeds are used to pay for some awesome work. My body's in peak physical condition. If it sells calendars or magazines to pay for machines to help sick kids or provide disaster relief, then I'm happy to help. I have a lot of fans, Carly. I won't deny it, but I only give my attention to those I want. You have my attention."

The words soothed the sting somewhat, but Carly's insecurities weren't so easily swayed. She didn't know where she would fit into his hockey life. It wasn't a trust issue as much as playing second fiddle to the best game on the planet.

"You're an amazing guy." She reached onto the tips of her toes and kissed him. The only remedy for her anxiety was his lips; his tongue; him.

But would that be enough?

He picked her up, and she wrapped her legs around his waist. The kiss deepened. The loud roar of an engine and the crackle of snow under tires broke the silence.

They both held their breath, waiting to confirm the sound. The engine turned off, and in the next instant, one and then another door closed.

Carly was panicking inside. What the heck were they going to do? There was no place to hide.

CHAPTER FIFTEEN

Theo put her back on the ground. "Someone's home."

Carly exhaled. It wasn't her overactive imagination. "Shit." She bent down and searched for the clothing she'd dropped. They needed to get dressed and get the hell out of there. "Help me find my pants."

The lack of light and the dark colored carpet hid her missing garments well. She crawled towards the door. She was sure she'd dropped them when Theo had picked her up there.

They couldn't greet the owners dressed like they were. This was a nightmare.

"Got 'em." He held up her jeans and twirled her panties around his finger.

The front door opened and the stomping of boots made her hold her breath. Her stomach was in her throat and all she could hear was the loud thumping of her heart. They were so screwed.

They could try to make it out the back door, but Theo's keys were in his coat at the front door. Her boots and most of their clothes were in the living room. They wouldn't be able to sneak out and survive outside for long in the nude. She had to think of another option.

She rushed over and pulled on what she could but she was missing the top half of her outfit and one sock. Theo had nothing. He stood before her buck naked as the footsteps creaked through the house.

"What are we going to do?" Carly whispered, covering her breasts with her arms.

"Hello! Is someone in here? I see your car out there." A deep male voice yelled.

"Daddy, there's jackets hung here too. I'm scared," a female said.

Carly closed her eyes and started counting. One. The loud thump of heavy footsteps pounded again.

Two. Once she opened her eyes, this would all disappear and it would be just the two of them again. Three.

"Now's not the time to check out." Theo grabbed a fleece blanket off the bed and wrapped it around himself. He pulled her into the shelter, covering their bodies from view. "We need to go introduce ourselves."

"This can't be happening." She closed the blanket, making sure all the important parts weren't visible. She checked the window; the snow had tapered. If she hadn't been so wrapped up in Theo she might have noticed the storm had passed.

"The longer we wait the more freaked they'll be." He cleared his throat and guided them towards the hall. "We're coming out," he announced loud enough so they'd expect them.

Tucked against his chest they shuffled down the hall towards the living room. "We needed a place to wait out the blizzard," Carly said, hoping to alert the owners that they meant to harm.

It was too late. A shotgun greeted them when they rounded the corner. The owner pointed the barrel directly at them with his finger positioned on the trigger. One wrong move and they were toast. This was a holiday face-off she never saw coming.

The candlelight flickered behind the man and his daughter, providing enough light to know they were in deep trouble. "Breaking and entering is against the law. Put your hands up where I can see 'em." He kept the gun aimed at Carly's chest. "Bet you're wanted criminals or something. Did you come for my girl?"

The man wore a flannel checkered top like the farmers back home. It didn't make him less intimidating. Especially if he thought they were somehow involved with the recent disappearances she'd seen on the news. No wonder he was pointing a gun at them.

Carly's hands shook as she followed orders. The blanket opened and her bare chest revealed. The fleece landed at her feet. Luckily, Theo was standing behind her and they couldn't tell he was completely naked.

"Oh, hell! What were you two doing in my baby's room?" His eyes assessed their lack of clothing, and he shot them a disgusted look. His baby was probably thirteen or fourteen and old enough to draw her own conclusions. Carly glanced over her shoulder; unsure how to answer.

"I promise we mean no harm. We needed a

shelter from the storm. That's it," Theo said with his hands raised above his head. "If you let us grab our stuff we'll leave right now."

There was enough light for her to see the young girl's eyes widen. Carly kept one hand in the air and covered her chest with the other. "Please don't shoot us. We aren't criminals."

The daughter squealed and started jumping up and down. The high-pitched shriek hurt Carly's ears. "OMG! You're Theo Montagne. Daddy, move." She shook her father's arm and the gun waved at them. "You are my favorite hockey player," she said, stepping closer.

Carly could almost see the saliva dripping from the girl's mouth as she eyed Theo from top to bottom. The farmer looked even less pleased. "I don't care who they are; they broke into our home. They're dangerous, Cybil. You need to stay back."

"Could you lower the gun, Sir? We just want to get our clothes and go. We are unarmed, and I promise if you move aside we will be out of your hair in minutes."

They were going to be shot. Her stomach did several flips as she eyed the closest exit. The farmer didn't look happy, but he lowered the gun. "Grab you shit and get out!"

"Thank you, Sir." Theo threaded his fingers with Carly's free hand, and they moved together as one unit. He kept his back to the wall as they moved past the pair in the hall.

"No. You can't leave." Cybil stepped closer as she took something out of her pocket. "No one is going to believe me."

The flash went off on Cybil's phone. She

snapped several pictures before Carly could react. Her first instinct was to grab the phone, but the girl was too far away and standing next to a man with a gun. The only thing she could do was protect Theo by keeping her body in front of his, and hoping the girl didn't have a good angle to catch all of him.

The flashes followed them in to the living room. She took multiple pictures of them as they rummaged through the pile of discarded clothes. Carly handed Theo his underwear and pants. He dressed quickly.

Cybil reached down and grabbed Theo's sweater. "You have to autograph something for me. You guys are going to win the cup. I know it." She clung to the top like it was made of pure gold.

"Only if you erase all those pictures," he said passing Carly her bra and shirt.

"No way! Those are mine and I'll cherish them forever. This is the best Christmas." Her glee wasn't shared by the rest of them. She turned her body and snapped a couple of selfies with Theo in the background.

Being famous had some serious disadvantages. They finished dressing and she wanted to get out of there as quickly as possible. "I'm so sorry for intruding on your holidays. Can you give Theo his sweater so we can leave?" She held out her hand but Cybil didn't budge.

"Cybil, give the man his damn shirt." He hadn't put the gun down, but he was no longer aiming it at them. His daughter didn't comply.

Theo tried to hide his annoyance with a charming smile. "Cybil, if you erase the pictures I'll take some new ones with you and autograph whatever you want. How does that sound?"

Carly put on her coat, waiting for the teenager to do the right thing. It never happened. The girl yammered on about how great Theo was and how much she loved hockey. He took it in stride and tried to win her over. It would have been sweet if she wasn't holding them hostage with incriminating photos.

They could have stood there for hours and there was no way that kid was going to erase naked pictures of her idol. "Let's go." Carly handed Theo his jacket but it was clear he didn't want to leave without deleting those pictures. "It's a lost cause."

"Enough. Get out, and don't come back." The farmer opened the door and motioned for them to follow.

Short of begging her to give him the phone, Theo asked her one last time. She hugged him but kept her phone out of reach. In the end, the farmer slammed the door on them without Theo's top or the pictures. Theo put on his jacket and remote started his car. They wiped the pile of snow off the windshield in silence.

Carly was in shock.

CHAPTER SIXTEEN

They drove to the end of the driveway before Carly broke out laughing. "That was the craziest thing ever." The giggles wouldn't stop. The situation was too ridiculous.

"Why are you laughing? There is nothing amusing about what happened." Theo pounded the stirring wheel with his fist.

His reaction wasn't expected. "Come on. We were naked and had a gun pointed at us. Then a fan girl stole your clothes. It's hilarious." She laughed again, but stopped when Theo stopped the car.

He ran his fingers through his hair. "It's a disaster and the opposite of funny. Dammit, I never should have left without taking her phone. We should go back."

She put her hand on his thigh and squeezed. "The only way you were going to get that phone was out of her dead little fingers. She idolizes you. Her room was covered in pictures of you and the team.

She'll probably print them off and add them to her collection. What's the big deal?"

Theo shook his head. "You don't get it, but you will."

"You're overreacting. There were no charges pressed. We got out safe and sound. It's a crazy story we should be able to laugh about. I mean, that could have ended so much worse." She reached up and gripped his chin, tilting his face towards her. "Theo, why does this bother you so much?"

His eyes caught hers and she could see the worry there. "As soon as she gets service back, she'll post those pictures all over her social media. Then it will go viral because I can't sneeze without getting press. Naked pictures of us will be everywhere. You thought dating a hockey player was going to be tough; now add media frenzy."

How could she have been so naïve? Of course, Cybil was old enough to post those pictures and tell her story. She might even sell the pictures.

"Balls! That sucks big harry ones."

Theo laughed, and he leaned into her hand. "You are amazing." He kissed her palm and Carly swooned. "Thanks for making me laugh, but do you think you can handle it?"

This big strong man was afraid of what this would mean for her. If she wasn't sure before, she was now. She loved him. "You were fighting to get the phone because you were worried about me?"

He chewed his lip and took a moment to answer. "Yeah, I don't want to scare you off. The limelight doesn't bother me. My reps might not like it but I don't care what they think about me. I care what you think."

"Theo—"

"Don't run from me. Whatever happens, we'll handle it together." He kissed her hand again.

Together. She liked the sound of that and her feet were firmly planted. "I'm not running. The idea of being plastered all over some tabloids wasn't on my bucket list but I think I can find a way to deal with it."

He breathed a sigh of relief. "I thought maybe you'd think I wasn't worth the hassle. I told you being with me would be complicated, but I'd hoped to ease you into it."

"Life is the complicated part. Being with you is easy." She leaned over the console and kissed him. As long as he kept kissing her like this she could handle anything.

"Let's get you home." Theo put the car back in gear and eased on the gas.

There was so much she wanted to say. Instead, she nodded and looked out the window. Whatever pictures surfaced they would face them together as a couple.

Theo maneuvered the car back onto the road and they inched slowly towards the highway. The road was impossible to see with the giant drifts. Carly didn't mind the soft hum of the Christmas carols on the radio. She found herself singing along with Theo to more than one. The longer she sat there watching him drive, the deeper she fell. There was too much to love about him. His arrogance had even grown on her.

She needed to tell him how she felt. He'd been honest about his feelings and she wanted to do the same. She opened her mouth to speak but the car stopped moving. She looked over and Theo's brows knitted together. That was not a good sign. "What's wrong?"

The tires spun, but the car refused to make progress. Carly could see the highway turn-off ahead, but there were no houses nearby. They hadn't seen another vehicle yet. "I think we're stuck," he said as he tried to rock the car off the snow drift.

He pushed his door open and snow tumbled inside. The car was buried in a mountain of snow. They forgot to grab a shovel for a moment like this, and the house was now miles away. "I'll try to push," she said, getting out and sinking into the white stuff. "Shit." She trudged her way to the back of the car. There was no way they were getting it out. Pushing with all her might didn't help them move an inch. If anything, it dug them in deeper.

"Switch!" Theo joined her. "You drive and I'll push."

"All right, but I don't think even your brute strength can get us out of his jam." They exchanged positions, but the results were the same.

After several wasted minutes, they huddled into the car to warm up. Theo blew on his hands to warm them. "I'm sorry. I couldn't see this drift. It—"

Carly reached over and squeezed his hand. "Totally not your fault. I don't blame you. You brought us to the highway; maybe we'll be able to flag someone down."

The suggestion they walk wasn't met with glowing reviews by Theo. He argued they were safer to wait. His plan was warmer, but she wanted to at least try. It was after midnight, and the likelihood of someone turning off the highway onto the remote country road wasn't great.

Logic won. Reluctantly, Theo agreed, and they ambled together to the main highway. He kept her tucked against him as they climbed drifts higher than her head. She was winded by the time they reached the road.

"Think anyone will come by?" Theo's nose was red, and he sniffled.

Carly was chilled to the bone and regretted her decision to get help. Her teeth chattered. "They better. Soon people will leave the parties and go home. Christmas is over." As she finished the sentence headlights appeared in the distance. "Look!"

"Sweet." Theo brushed a frozen kiss against her lips. "We'll be safe and warm in no time."

Visibility had improved dramatically from the day before, but it was hard to gauge the distance in the dark. Neither of them had worn anything reflective or bright to signal their presence to the driver. They waved their hands in the air, trying to alert them that they needed help. Based on the position of the lights Carly guessed it was a car. The driver kept changing lanes, swerving all over the highway.

Theo stood closer to the road as the car neared. Carly didn't have a good feeling. Instead of slowing down, it sounded as if the car revved its engine, picking up speed. People often say there's a moment of clarity before disaster strikes. All Carly saw was two bright lights turn and point directly at them. In that second, her only thought was of Theo and his safety. She gripped his jacket and yanked with all her might. He stumbled backwards behind her towards the ditch. Then she heard a loud screeching of break as the lights blinded her. Pain spread across her side and it felt like she was flying.

CHAPTER SEVENTEEN

C arly wanted to open her eyes but the most alluring dream lingered in the forefront of her mind. She pictured the famous hockey player's face with precision detail. Dark blue eyes, framed by long thick lashes; strong jaw, dusted with stubble; and the most sensual full lips perfect for kissing. She could almost feel his kiss. Her lips tingled at the fading memory.

She expected to open her eyes and be in the darkness of her dorm room, instead she was greeted by bright overhead lights. The last remnants of sleep disappeared, and she blinked until her eyes adjusted to the brightness. They burned while her lids fought to remain closed.

"You're awake." Carly recognized the soft melodic tone of her mother's voice. The short woman rushed to Carly's side and gripped her hand hard.

"Are you okay? Let me get the doctor. Stan, go fetch the doctor."

Carly was confused why she needed to see a doctor. She felt fine. Her parents had always been the over-protective type. One of the side effects from being an only child.

"I'm fine, Mom." She tried to sit up, but her mother pushed her back into the bed with a firm hand to the shoulder. Carly looked at her mom and noticed the red, puffy eyes, and runny nose. A strong indication she'd been crying.

"You are most certainly not fine. You almost died." Her mother sobbed and dropped her head onto Carly's chest. "I don't know what... I would do if I lost you too."

Everything in her mind sped by in a blur of information, slightly out of reach. She felt dizzy. She ran her fingers through her mother's silver hair, reassuring her she was okay. But she wasn't okay, because she was lying in a hospital bed.

"What happened?" The words came out slightly slurred. She was tired, keeping her eyes open was a difficult task to accomplish.

"You don't remember?" A familiar, deep masculine voice said from somewhere in the room.

Carly sought the sound and feasted upon the man of her dreams. Theo Montagne was sitting in a chair, looking every bit as sexy as he did on television. Only he became fuzzy and the room behind him spun.

"The room is moving too fast." Carly couldn't concentrate. She closed her eyes to keep from getting sick, only it didn't help. Her stomach was ready to revolt at any moment.

"Miss Saint, I'm Doctor Patel. You were struck by a car and admitted for a head injury and some minor lacerations."

She opened her eyes and attempted to zero in on the doctor but failed. "What?" Her hands moved over the bandages on her head.

"You're lucky there were no major injuries from the impact other than some bumps and bruises. The snow must have softened your landing but you were knocked unconscious. We sedated you while we assessed, cleaned and stitched the cuts on your scalp. You may feel groggy for another moment or two, but it will pass. You've been out for several hours. How do you feel?"

The doctor spoke quickly. It made her head hurt. The longer they spoke the more the pain set in. Her entire body ached.

"I feel like I was hit by a car. Everything hurts. What time is it?" She tried to sit up again but winced in agony. Theo rounded the bed and rubbed her back. His fingers caressed her cheek. The gesture was sweet, but she didn't want him to see her like this. Vulnerable and weak.

"It's early evening. Do you remember anything?" Theo asked.

Carly had been unconscious for an entire day, but she recalled every moment of her time with Theo. The past few days had been the best of her life. Until an idiot rammed into her on the side of the highway. "It will take more than being run over by a car to forget you."

A shiver of unease raced down her spine when she thought about how she almost lost him. She eyed him from top to bottom, checking for any wounds.

He looked perfect.

The doctor gave her a reassuring smile. "We will have to keep you overnight to monitor your concussion. We should be able to release you in the morning. The scan revealed no broken bones, but you'll have some discomfort." He cleared his throat before continuing. "Do you have any questions?"

The questions she had weren't for the doctor. "Are you sure we can't take her home tonight?" Carly's father patted her foot, and she burst into tears at the sight of him. He wore his favorite NHL team hat, which also happened to be Theo's team. His warm smile brought back so many memories.

"It's standard protocol I'm afraid. First thing tomorrow morning is the best we can do."

She did not understand how her parents arrived, but she was thankful. Her dad came to her side and took the hand she was using to hide her tears. "Hush, girl, everything will be okay." She drew strength from their support.

The doctor made his exit, drawing the curtain closed while the tears fell. Her mother cried right along with her. Even her dad looked on the verge of letting the waterworks fly. He was the rugged outdoorsman who rarely showed emotion. She never doubted his love, because he said the words often, but he wasn't a sentimental guy.

Nothing like a near death experience to bring a family together. "I'm so sorry I didn't take an earlier flight." This mess was avoidable. "I wanted us to be together for the holidays, but not like this." Her joke made them all laugh.

"We're together now," her mother said, patting her leg.

Carly reached out and took Theo's hand. "Thank you. How did you pull this off? How did you get them here?"

"It was nothing. They needed to be here. You need your family." His modesty made her heart swell. He kissed her knuckles.

She'd been falling for him from the moment she met him, but his kindness sealed the deal. She loved Theo for who he was on the inside, not the hockey or the perfect smile. There was no such thing as perfect, but Theo came darn close.

"Yes, we can't thank you enough, Mr. Montagne. No parent ever wants to get a call that her baby's been in an accident, and it's worse when she's thousands of miles away. But you got us here. You're a miracle worker," her mother said, as she walked over to Theo. She pulled him into her arms and hugged him tight.

Theo shuffled his feet uncomfortably, but hugged her back. "No thanks are needed as I told you before, but you're most welcome. I suppose I should leave you all." He turned to face Carly and his forehead creased like he had something important to say. But he said nothing.

"Please don't go." She smiled, and he returned the gesture. "Mom and Dad, do you mind giving us a moment alone?"

"Of course, darling." Her mother kissed her cheek and took her dad's hand, lacing their fingers together. Over twenty-five years of marriage and they were still head over heels in love. It made Carly hopeful for a future like that someday. Maybe she had a chance at happily ever after too.

"Merry Christmas, sweet-pea." Her father leaned

down and kissed her forehead. She'd always been daddy's little girl and nothing would ever change that. "You make your mother and I so proud. Every day we thank our lucky stars to have you, Carly."

She hugged her dad with all her might, which at the moment wasn't much. "I love you too, Daddy."

Once the door closed, she patted the bed beside her.

"You saved my life." Theo crawled into the bed next to her and pulled her into his arms. He was careful not to squeeze her too hard. "When I found you knocked-out in a snow bank, I thought I might lose you. There was so much blood and you weren't talking to me. I'm not afraid to admit I've never been so scared in my entire life."

"I was terrified when the car swerved towards us. But you can't afford to be injured." She may have pushed him out of the way and saved him, but he'd saved her in so many ways.

She wrapped her arms around him, ready to never let go. "How did we get here?"

"The car that hit you ended up skidding off the road but stayed out of the ditch. The stupid jerk had been texting while driving. I carried you to his car and made him drive us to the nearest hospital. If he wasn't so sorry for his actions I might have killed him with my bare hands. You almost died."

She squeezed him harder. "But I didn't."

"We got lucky. After you were admitted, I had my PA locate your family and fly them here. We've been waiting a while for you to come around. It's been a long day," he said, stifling a yawn.

"That's crazy. Are you okay? Did the car hit you too? Have you been here the whole time?" She wanted to know everything that happened.

Theo pressed a kiss to the top of her head. "Hell yeah, I've been here the entire time. I wasn't leaving you, Carly. Nothing happened to me thankfully. Other than some bruises from being thrown into the ditch; I'm fine. How are you?"

"I don't know. I'm still processing this, but I'm so happy to be alive and to have you. Why are you still here? Not that I'm not happy you're here; I am. It's just...I thought you had hockey every day for the next little while."

Theo nodded. "I couldn't leave you. I called my people and I'll make it work. Your health and safety is all that matters."

He picked her over hockey. She smiled so big the room couldn't contain it. They held each other for a few minutes, enjoying the closeness. Carly was afraid to let go.

"What happens next, Theo? I mean, between us." Her heart rate increased with her nerves. It was embarrassing since the monitor beeped, giving her secrets away.

He lifted her chin and kissed her lips. A feather light kiss; both promising and tender. "Carly, I told you, I'm falling in love with you. What do you want to see in your future?"

"You." One word that held so much potential.

"I'm glad you said that because I love you. I'm yours, today and tomorrow, there's no expiration date on my love."

Carly laughed at how corny her boyfriend was. Her boyfriend.

"I've fallen too. I love you, Theo. Does this make me your girlfriend?" She liked the sound of it rolling off her tongue, and she hoped he liked it too.

He smiled; the panty-melting smile that stole her heart. "It sure does, and for the record, I plan to keep my Christmas present forever."

"I'm yours." She leaned in to kiss him but something vibrated against her leg. Theo reached between them and checked his phone. His brows knitted together. Whatever he'd read wasn't good news. "Is everything okay?"

"Nothing my PR team can't handle. I'll keep you posted though."

Carly suspected it had something to do with the pictures of them, but couldn't be sure. She expected difficulties along the way. Dating a pro-hockey player wouldn't be a cake walk, but Theo was worth it. They'd take it one day and one game at a time.

His mouth covered hers and this time when their lips met it wasn't light. It was brutal and honest, leaving nothing behind. The past was in the past, and they were moving forward—together.

$\mathcal{E}$PILOGUE

After Theo left, Carly wasn't sure what to make of everything that had happened. Part of her was elated to have him in her corner, but she was nervous. He was everything she wanted in a man, and everything she hated.

"Theo seems like a really nice young man. It was very generous of him to get us a hotel so close to the hospital," her mother said, taking a seat in the uncomfortable metal chair next to her. They waited for the doctor to sign her release papers.

Her mother's words weren't enough. Nice didn't fit Theo. He was so much more than that. Her love for him was all so new, but it felt right. "Theo's a wonderful man, Mom. I'm damn lucky he came along when he did."

That much she knew for sure. If Theo hadn't come out of the diner when he did, she'd have ended up in a worse way. Those men could have done anything to her. Then he saved her life by bring her to the hospital. He saved her from years of loneliness. She swallowed and closed her eyes.

Her mother took her hand and squeezed. "Your father and I couldn't thank him enough. But you never should have been in that situation. Not to mention all those pictures of you two online. Goodness gracious; this city is full of horrible people. Won't you come home?"

Carly rolled her eyes at her mother's plea. The moment Theo left, they had pounced on her to return back to their small town. Where things were safer. Where people didn't spread gossip. She disagreed. Bad things happened everywhere, and she loved her new city, her school and Theo.

"I belong here. And I think I looked pretty good in most of the shots." Her smile was met with a stern eyebrow lift. The kind only a mother can deliver.

The pictures had indeed gone viral just as Theo predicted. Except, she didn't care. He went out of his way to get his team on it, trying to stop sites from sharing and posting. But once things are online and out in the world the damage is done. Carly joked about it being their coming out announcement. Theo was officially off the market and now the entire world knew it. She couldn't be upset about that.

She also didn't hate that Theo stayed at the hospital with her all day, missing his practice. Her new boyfriend had refused to leave her side. They talked for hours. He would have spent the night, but he had a plane to catch. Saying goodbye had been much harder than she expected. In a short amount of time, Theo Montagne, had wormed his way into her heart.

Her father stepped next to her, holding papers in

his hand. "We are good to go. I'd prefer it if you came to the hotel with us. At least for tonight."

"Please, Carly," her mother begged. They didn't want to leave her alone, and truthfully, she was happy to be near them. She might not have wanted to go back home with them, but she had missed them terribly. Family meant everything to Carly.

The concussion was mild, but her head still hurt like crazy. Bruises covered most of the right side. The silver lining was that she was alive and would live to see another sunrise. "Sounds good. Let's get out of here."

"Are you Carly Saint?" A young nurse wearing pink scrubs ran up to her. Carly nodded as she rose to her feet with a little help from her dad. "This package came for you. Have a great day," she said, handing her a white plastic courier bag, before taking off down the hall.

Carly ripped it open and found three tickets to Theo's next hockey game. The away game that was taking him away for the next few days. Behind those, were three return plane tickets and a box of chocolates. She hugged the contents against her chest. His generosity blew her away, but it was too much.

"What's inside?" Her father leaned over her shoulder.

She couldn't contain her delight. "Tickets to tomorrow's NHL game for all three of us. In New York!" She'd be seeing Theo sooner than expected.

Her parents were taken aback by his kindness and they spent the short cab ride to the hotel discussing the upcoming game and Theo's hockey prowess. The man had many talents and Carly was eager to explore them all.

When they got to the hotel, her parents changed into their bathing suits and headed down to the hot tub for some relaxation time. Carly figured they were leaving to give her some time to rest, but she was too excited to sleep.

The moment the door closed behind them, she picked up her phone and called Theo. His clean-shaven face appeared on her screen. He looked handsome as always, but she missed the scruff. "You are amazing!"

He chuckled at her greeting. His brown hair covered his left eye in a disheveled yet sexy way. "You got my gift I take it, or am I amazing for another reason." He waggled his thick brows.

Oh, there were many reasons, but she didn't need to inflate his ego. "I love my present, and my folks are excited to catch the game too. They can't stop talking about playoffs and how this is going to be the year. But you didn't have to do this. I mean it's way too much. Once they come back from the pool, we'll look into hotels. I bet—"

"Don't. It's all taken care of. My assistant looked after everything; a car will take you to the airport first thing tomorrow morning and another will take you to my hotel. I like that your folks have confidence in the team. Playoffs are still months away but if we keep playing good we've got a shot. I know it's a little much, but I couldn't wait till New Year's Eve to see you again. Please don't think of this as a big deal. This is my way of getting to know my future in-laws and spending time with my girl. How are you feeling?"

He was so damn thoughtful. And he said in-laws?

Carly couldn't wait to be with him again too. "I feel like kissing you. That's how I feel."

Theo laughed again. The sound tickled her insides. Then, he covered his screen as she overheard him, excusing himself from those around him. A minute later, things got quiet and his handsome face reappeared. "Sorry about that. I'm at the rink, waiting to see one of the trainers. There was too much noise to hear you properly, but I'm alone now. Can you tell me again how you feel?" His voice took on that deep timber she loved and his blue eyes sparkled with desire.

"You heard me. I want to be kissing you right now. I miss you. Is that strange?" She chewed her lip, waiting for his response.

"Are you alone, Carly?"

She tilted her phone to show Theo her surroundings. The beige walls and brown bedspread weren't fancy, but the hotel was clean and had all the modern amenities you'd expect. "Yes, I'm in my parent's hotel room, lying on the bed." She rolled onto her side.

He growled and her insides quivered. "I wish I was in that bed with you. If you haven't already, put the phone down cause you're going to use your hands for me."

She liked where he was going with this. "Okay." Her voice sounded breathless as she propped the phone on the pillow.

"Take your clothes off. I want to see your gorgeous naked body. Are you wet, Carly?" His voice alone made her panties damp.

"Yes. Where are you?" She ran to the door and used the chain to lock it in case her parents came to check on her. Then she made sure Theo got a good view of her taking off her top and bra. He raked his teeth over his lower lip, and over the small scar she loved. So sexy.

Carly removed the rest of her clothes and lay facing him on the bed. She draped her arm over her side, trying to cover the bruises. When she looked into his eyes, she observed nothing but passion and love. She moved her arm and let him see all of her. She had nothing to hide.

He moved the angle of his phone so she saw more than his face. Theo was in a private bathroom stall and his jeans were open. She watched him reach inside and pull out his thick, long cock. It was hard. "If you were here, I'd have you on your knees sucking this right now." He stroked his length as he spoke. "Instead, I'll use my hand and watch you use yours. You're so damn beautiful. Pick up your phone and show me how wet your pussy is."

Carly would have liked nothing more than to be with him, pleasing him. So, she did as he asked and moved the phone between her open legs, giving him a perfect shot of her arousal. He did that to her. She watched his eyes widen, and it turned her on even more.

"You are so damn hot. I wish I was touching you right now and licking that moisture from the tip of your cock. What else do you want me to do?" She was panting already, and she'd barely done anything.

He smiled. A devilish grin that made her legs quiver. "You like my cock. Don't you, Carly?" His hand moved faster as she nodded. "Good. Use one hand to pinch your pretty pink nipple. If I were there, it would be in my mouth already. Then use your other hand to make yourself come. Dip two or three fingers inside that tight little slice of heaven."

Carly followed orders and moaned when she felt her arousal, coating her fingers.

"That's perfect and I can hear the suction of your pussy begging for more. Pump those fingers to the same speed as my hand and use your thumb against your clit. My balls are tightening, remembering how good it feels to be inside you."

The faster she worked her body, the closer she came to the brink of ecstasy. Carly remembered how great it felt to be filled by him too. "I love you, Theo," she said. Those words, and the sight of him nearing his release thrust her into an orgasmic state of happiness.

They spent the next fifteen minutes talking about the most deliciously naughty things. He made her blush in places she hadn't dreamed could turn red. And best of all, he made her come again before he shot his load all over his hand.

She didn't want to let him go, but he had people to see and hockey to play.

"I'll see you tomorrow, sweetheart. I love you." Theo hung up and Carly counted the hours until they would be together again.

Phone sex was new to her, but she had a feeling they would have many more moments like that in the future. Theo would be busy trying to win the Stanley Cup but she knew he'd make time for her. His team needed him but so did she.

It was funny to think about having a future with a hockey-superstar because Carly had been adamant about staying away from men who played the sport. But as with most things in life, she could adapt. Carly was a smart girl; too intelligent to let the best man walk out of her life. Theo was a keeper, and she intended on making their relationship work.

Loving a hockey player would have its share of drawbacks, but a strong woman like Carly could handle any situation. In hockey, there's no such thing as a perfect season. When she looked into the future, she could see her happily ever after, and it was damn close to perfect.

$\mathscr{P}$OKE $\mathscr{C}$HECKING

The next book in Kristen Echo's Puck Battle Series.

Follow the team as they play their hearts out in their quest for the Stanley Cup and for love.

Loving a hockey player is against the rules. But some rules were meant to be broken.
Caroline was used to taking all kinds of risks. When she told her father that she wanted to quit University to become a musician, he supported her and landed her band a gig on New Year's Eve. His only condition was that she couldn't date a hockey player.
Easy.
Except one foolish game turned her world upside-down.
One perfectly sinful night caused her to break all the rules.
Nicolas wasn't just any hockey player; he was the team captain. A leader on the ice and between the sheets. She couldn't walk away.
Their secret relationship had the power to ruin more than two lives. Her decisions had the power to destroy her heart and an entire team. But damn, he was worth the risk.

Each book in the Puck Battle series features a different couple and can be read as a standalone. HEA guaranteed.

Author Note

Thank you for reading Holiday Face-off. I had a blast writing it, and I hope you had fun reading it.

If you didn't get enough of Theo and Carly then head over to my website and check out the bonus content area where you can claim your extended epilogue. It's exclusively available to members of my mailing list. Subscribe and get access to all the bonus content.

I would be honored and grateful if you chose to leave a review. I read all my reviews and enjoy getting feedback about my writing. If you want more hockey stories then please leave a review, and let me know you love the series and can't wait for more.

ABOUT THE AUTHOR

Kristen Echo is a lover of romance stories. She writes passionate love stories that are both sexy and dirty. Her books will make you feel more than a little naughty in all the right places.

She lives in Manitoba, Canada where she spends any free time with her two lovely little girls and the love of her life. When she's not writing, you can find her contemplating life's mysteries with her hands wrapped around a cup of coffee, or with her nose stuck in a sizzling hot romance.

The Puck Battle Series is a sports romance series and as mentioned, she's a Canadian, so of course she loves hockey. The Winnipeg Jets are her home team and will forever hold a special place in her heart. But her true love is football. Sorry, Canadian Football League—she's a diehard NFL fan. Blue and orange are her colors.

Stay connected with Kristen at:
Website: www.echoromance.com
Facebook: www.facebook.com/authorkristenecho
Goodreads: www.goodreads.com/KristenEcho